ALLEN COUNTY PUBLIC LIBRARY
3 1833 00702
FRIENDS OF ACPL
W9-BCD-476

Desert Stallion

DESERT STALLION

by

HOBART DONAVAN

ILLUSTRATED BY WILLIAM RILEY

ALFRED A. KNOPF: NEW YORK

1966

00 028

79 10672 2

L.C. catalog card number: 53-7631

THIS IS A BORZOI BOOK,
PUBLISHED BY ALFRED A. KNOPF, INC.

COPYRIGHT 1953 BY HOBART DONAVAN. All rights reserved. No part of this book may be reproduced in any form without permission in writing from the publisher, except by a reviewer who may quote brief passages and reproduce not more than three illustrations in a review to be printed in a magazine or newspaper. Manufactured in the United States of America and distributed by Random House, Inc. Published simultaneously in Toronto, Canada, by Random House of Canada, Ltd.

Published, August 1953
Second printing, January 1959
Third printing, March 1966

1431069

TO

Jim, Mary Ann, AND *Colleen*

WHO LEARNED MUCH ABOUT LIFE

FROM OUR HORSES

Desert Stallion

Chapter 1

THE HOT WIND blew sand in little twinkling lines across the desert floor, like so many brown snakes, running in and out between the feet of the Arab boy who stood gazing with worshipful eyes at the crest of a sand dune a few hundred feet away. The same wind ruffled the mane and tail of the great grey stallion that stood like a carved statue on the crest of the dune watching the boy. Saya held out his hand, and he spoke almost soundlessly.

"Khala Hawa," he whispered. "Wind of the desert. That is what I shall always call you!"

Almost as though he understood, though he could not have heard the boy's whisper, the great horse reared high on his hind legs, spun about, and galloped away over the crest of the dune. So easily did he run, and so rapidly, that he seemed to float through the air like the wind. Saya watched for the moment it took the horse to disappear, then he sighed and returned to his father's goat-hair tent pitched in the shade of tall date palms in the nearby oasis.

Sheik Akim Abou . . . for Saya's father was sheik of their Bedouin tribe . . . looked up as Saya entered the tent and watched his son for a moment. Then he said:

"Eat of the bread and cheese my son. A man without food is no man at all."

Saya smiled fondly at his father.

"Thank you my father," he said. "But the hunger I have is not for food."

Sheik Abou narrowed his eyes.

"Saya," he said. "I think I know the hunger you have. You have lived now for twelve times twelve months. Perhaps you are ready to grow up."

Saya smiled again. "I had not thought of that father. I am content."

His father stood up.

"Come my son," he said. "I know what to do for the boy who has the look which is in your eyes."

Akim Abou rose gracefully to his feet from the camel

saddle against which he had been leaning to eat his evening meal. He was a tall man, lean and hard-muscled. Far and wide over the desert he was known as a just man, but a man ready to defend himself and his people in whatever way was necessary. His hawk-like face was brown, the olive skin tanned to an even darker shade by the burning desert sun. But now a smile drew aside the spade beard which curtained his lips, and his eyes which could narrow into hard brown slits twinkled as he looked down at the strong, serious son who meant so much to him. He strode from the tent motioning to Saya to follow him, and the two walked across the green of the oasis. Beyond the tall palm trees the desert was visible, but here in the oasis, it was easy to imagine if one did not look toward the sand dunes that the desert was far away. Once outside the tent, Akim Abou did not hurry. He walked slowly so that the shorter legs of his son could match his long stride; nor did he speak to the boy, but instead watched him carefully though seeming not to do so. In fact, Akim Abou was just a little puzzled at the strange actions of his son, who, though he seemed perfectly happy, obviously had something on his mind. Soon they came to the herd of horses which grazed on tender grasses and shrubs. Now again the soft light came into the Sheik's eyes as he looked at the handsome beasts, for there is no horse in the world more beautiful than the classic Arabian. And indeed, every fine horse in the world today owes his speed, beauty and endurance to famous Arabian stallions that lived over two hundred years ago. Akim Abou pointed to the graceful animals.

"See them Saya. Are they not wonderful creatures? There is no horse in the world as fine as the horse of Arabia. And of these, the Bedouins' . . . ours . . . are the finest."

Saya looked wistful. "Yes father," he answered. "They are beautiful. Strong and beautiful. I love them all."

Sheik Abou laid his hand on the boy's shoulder.

"Pick the one you want to own, my son. Any one except my war-mare, Baku."

Saya turned away. His eyes looked toward the crest of the sand dune where the great wild stallion had stood.

"I want none of them my father. I am content to ride the old ones you no longer use."

Akim Abou looked at him in amazement.

"My son! Surely I did not hear you correctly. You, the one boy in our camp who rides better than most men. You . . . the only one besides myself who can ride my great mare Baku! You do not want a horse of your own?"

Saya looked appealingly at his father.

"I do want a horse of my own father. More than anything I want a horse. But these horses I do not want."

"Surely you do not mean these great horses are not good enough for you? Look you Saya. That bay mare! Five years old, fast as the wind. Would you not like to own her? Any man in our camp would give his tent and his rifle for her!"

Saya dug his toe in the sand and answered hesitantly.

"No father. She is a nice mare. Often have I ridden her. But I do not want to own her."

The Sheik was puzzled. "My son," he said, "there

are many men who can ride a horse as though they grew in the saddle. There are many men who can handle even the most dangerous horse with ease. But every once in a while some person appears who seems almost kin to the horse. Such a man is worshipped by the horses. For him they will do anything. You are like that."

Saya answered slowly.

"I have known that, father. And it has made me happy."

Akim Abou nodded. He was pleased at this wisdom in his son.

"It is well you know the great blessing Allah has bestowed on you. Now my son, select a horse for yourself. And someday your name will be on every tongue, in every part of the world where horses are known and loved. Which of the horses do you want?"

Saya was miserable. He loved his father and his father loved him. He knew that what he was about to say would make his father unhappy, yet, he had to say it. He raised his head and spoke slowly but with determination.

"My father, please do not be unhappy with me. None of these horses are for me. There is only one horse in the desert I would own. He is the great grey stallion, the wild horse, whom I call Khala Hawa, Wind of the Desert."

Akim Abou was astounded!

"What?" he cried. "The wild stallion who raids our herds and leads away our best mares?"

Saya was shamed. "Y-yes father, he is the one. But oh, father, he is fast as the desert wind. If your mare is as two horses, the great grey one is as ten horses! Such great muscles, such a tremendous chest! Such power! Father, he does not run, he floats, as does a cloud in the sky!"

The Sheik's eyes looked far off in the distance and he seemed to see a powerful grey stallion, his body muscled for speed and endurance such as no other horse could match. In his mind also he saw himself mounted on this great horse, he felt the surge of the powerful legs, the rippling of the chest muscles, the impact of this magnificent creature against the wind which constantly stirred the sand of the desert, and he felt this wind hard against his face, felt his long white burnoose whipping about his shoulders as it streamed out behind their flying figures. Then with a frown he dismissed the thought. But his thoughts had told him how his son felt, and it was with a sorrowful expression that he said kindly to Saya:

"Saya, I know the horse. He is perhaps the greatest of all horses in Arabia. But he is wild, the son of a wild mother. He will never be tamed."

Saya's jaw grew firm.

"Someday I hope to find a way, father."

"Then I must sadden you with this. Again and again

the wild stallion has galloped through our camps at night. Again and again he has stolen from us fine mares from our herd. Tomorrow our men go to hunt him for they are angered. And when we find him we must kill him."

The new day dawned in typical desert splendor. The sun climbed high early in the sky, a fiery red ball which would soon bake the sand until the dunes danced with waves of heat. But the small oasis, watered by the bubbling spring, remained fairly comfortable. The tall date palms thrust upward like long fingers, their fronds warding off the lancing sun rays and shielding the clusters of ripe fruit which hung below the green branches. A few birds made cheerful music as they flew about the little paradise in mid-desert and many insects buzzed and droned in the pleasant shade.

All of this was lost upon Saya. He went about his work with bowed head, for in his mind thoughts of the great wild stallion that came to their camp to stand like a grey statue carved from marble, looking down at him, crowded out all else. He thought of what his father had said and, being a desert boy, he understood fully what happened to wild stallions that raided the Arab's herds and lured away the valuable mares. His father was determined that Khala Hawa be killed. The mind of the boy throbbed as he milked his goats and his thoughts kept time with his flying hands.

"They will kill him. They will kill him. They will kill him."

As he leaped lightly onto the back of an old mare to herd the horses to their pasture the thudding hooves seemed to pick up the words and the plodding walk of the old mare repeated them.

"They will kill him. They will kill him. They will kill him."

As he watched the horses at their grazing, his mind pictured again the magnificent grey stallion, neck arched, legs tense, hooves seeming to barely rest on the sand. He saw the luxurious white mane and tail floating on the desert wind for which he had named the horse. And then in his mind he heard the sharp crack of a rifle, he listened tensely to the whine of the bullet. He felt the sickening impact of the bullet as the lead struck the shining side of the wild stallion. He saw the great grey horse leap high in the air and then collapse on the ground as the bullet found its way into his vitals. Saya clenched his hands tightly. Beads of sweat stood out upon his face as his imagination ran away with him. He heard the last gasping breath of the beautiful wild horse as it slowly poured its life-blood on the sand. Then Saya leaped suddenly to his feet, shaking and white faced.

"It must not happen! My father must not kill Khala Hawa!"

Slowly Saya returned to his senses. Well he knew the grim law of the desert. The transgressor must die! And the wild stallion was a criminal. Often had the grey horse raided the herds of the Arabs to lead away mares to share his own wild life. Khala Hawa must die! Saya's own father said it. And here came the men of the camp to fetch their horses and, as his father had decided, to follow the grey stallion and kill him. Now Saya faced reality. His head remained bowed as the men caught up horse after horse, to place on them the tasseled Bedouin bridles and their saddles. When the men swung onto their horses' backs, drew their burnooses tightly about themselves to ward off the desert heat, gripped their slim, long rifles firmly, and rode to their places in the line, Saya still did not raise his head. But when the men spread out over the desert in a long column of twos, Saya lifted his head for one look, then threw himself down on the sparse grass to sob in his misery.

It was thus that Nedda found him. Nedda was sweet and tiny, and Saya loved this little sister very much. Nedda in turn adored this big brother of hers, and envied him each time he jumped to the back of one of the tribe's fleet horses, to speed across the desert sands. The little girl wondered at the sorrow which made her brother sob, but she sat down beside him and waited patiently until he quieted. Then she spoke.

"What saddens my brother?"

Saya raised a tear stained face and tried a little smile, but it disappeared as quickly as it came. His voice was low as he told Nedda,

"Nedda," he said, "our father rides with his men to kill the grey stallion. I am saddened, because this horse I love. If only I could come close to him and speak to him and touch him. Then he would not do the bad things which make him an outlaw now."

Nedda nodded her pretty little head.

"Mother told me of the wild stallion. He is like a bad man. He comes among our horses and steals the mares. This morning two more mares have run off with him, and the young stallion belonging to Emal Dukka is badly hurt. They fought, you see."

Saya wiped away the tears with his sleeve. Then for a long moment his eyes searched the desert which stretched endlessly beyond the oasis. Now, turning back to Nedda he spoke.

"All this I know," he said. "But if I could make friends with the stallion he would not do these things. I would tell him not to do these things. But now it is too late. They ride to hunt him down and kill him."

Nedda's eyes, already large, grew larger.

"Saya," she asked. "Can you really tell the horse to

act in the good ways and he will understand you?"

Saya nodded.

"I do not know how, Nedda," he said. "It is not what I say, for the horses do not understand our words. But when I speak in a certain way the horses will do as I wish." Saya shook his head in puzzled fashion and continued. "Our father told me that some men are born kin to the horse and I am such a one. It may be so. This I do not know, but I do know that when I speak to a horse he seems to understand. It would be so with the grey one."

The dimples came and went in Nedda's round cheeks as suddenly a great idea occurred to her. To her mind the problem was simply solved.

"Quickly brother," she said. "Take a horse and ride after our father and the men. When they catch the grey one you can tell him not to do bad things and then they will not kill him."

Saya smiled at his little sister's suggestion but he sat up quickly and a new hope came into his eyes. Now he turned his head to look out over the broad expanse of sand. The brown waste seemed to stretch limitlessly and though it disappeared in the distance below the horizon, Saya knew that hundreds and hundreds of miles of dunes and wind-swept levels stretched beyond. His eyes narrowed as do the eyes of all desert men against the bright sun. Then slowly he rose to his feet. He looked down at his little sister and spoke.

"Come Nedda. I will take you back to our mother. Then, as you have said, I will take a horse and ride to my grey one. Who can tell? It may be that Allah in his goodness will permit us now to know each other.

Chapter 2

OVER THE DESERT sands Akim Abou and his men swept in a wild gallop. The swift horses urged on with heel and voice stretched out their fine legs until they seemed almost to fly. Yet, a half mile ahead of them running effortlessly, floated the grey stallion. On the crest of each dune he would halt, turn and watch the oncoming riders. He would rear high in the air, and strike with his sharp hooves in their direction as though warning them to keep their distance. Then turning, he would plunge down the sandy slope and bound across the sand playing his wild game of chase with the horsemen and enjoying every moment.

Sheik Akim Abou, riding his speedy Baku was a little distance ahead of his men. Again, far ahead of them, the huge grey horse halted on a high place and looked back. Abou held up his hand and reined Baku to a halt. His men galloped up and halted behind him. Abou spoke.

"Men, we wear our horses needlessly. We will never come closer to the wild stallion. See him. He stands on yonder dune and almost seems to laugh at us. He knows he can run all day and we will never catch him."

One of the men reined his mount close to the Sheik and spoke.

"Then there is only one thing to do. We must shoot from here."

Abou answered: "It is an order I hate to give."

The man spoke again: "Give no order. This is a far and difficult shot. No man can make it but yourself. Shoot, Akim Abou."

The Sheik bowed his head and answered.

"I cannot shoot him. The horse is loved by the son of my blood, nor have I the heart to destroy so much beauty. Emal Dukka, your stallion was hurt. You have a grudge to settle. It is your shot."

Emal Dukka sitting his horse a short distance away looked at the great stallion and quietly made his rifle ready.

"Abou, it is for me to try, but I think the distance is too much for my aim. Nevertheless, I will shoot first. Steady my sweet mount."

Even as Emal Dukka raised his long rifle, Saya, bending low over his horse's withers fairly flew over the ground. He followed the horsemen easily for the wind had not yet swept clear the marks of their horses' hooves. In Saya's heart was a great joy for he had convinced himself that he would at last come close to his beloved wild stallion. When his mount reached the crest of a dune, Saya saw the horsemen before him, and far away, posed on another dune, the grey stallion unhurt, standing proudly against the sky. His heart leaped with relief. And then, a rifle shot rang

out, and just as he had pictured it in his dream the grey stallion gave a great bound into the air, crashed to the earth and lay still in the sand.

Saya gave a cry of grief and pounded his heels into his mount's side. The horse snorting in surprise, leaped across the space to the riders.

The stallion thrashed his powerful legs in the sand and tried to rise, and Saya heard his father say:

"Look you. The stallion is not dead. We must ride closer and kill him mercifully."

Saya spurred his mount to a last burst of speed and drew rein near his father.

"Father, father! No, father!"

Akim Abou looked around in surprise as did all the men. Urging his horse close to his father's mount, the boy pleaded:

"Father! I have hurried but I may be too late, even so. Go away. Take the men with you. Let me go to the horse. If he suffers greatly, I . . . I will help him to die quickly. That at least I would like to have."

Akim Abou looked at the saddened face of his son and bowed his head.

"That I can give you my son. So great a horse must have a soul as do we. Go to your friend my son. Commend his soul to Allah's care. If you do not have him here, perhaps in another life he will carry you swiftly and safely."

For that was Akim Abou's belief, and so he motioned his men to follow him home. Saya slid down from his horse's back and slowly, sorrowfully walked to the great grey stallion. The boy knelt in the sand at the head of the splendid horse. The big eyes looked at him, unafraid, defiant, but the lifeblood of the magnificent animal streamed out onto the sand. Saya spoke to him:

"Grey one! Grey one! Do you hurt badly? Is there nothing Saya can do?"

The horse nickered softly. Perhaps he knew that soon he would be gone from this world of sand and sun and wind which he had ruled so bravely only a few moments ago. Perhaps, thinking this, he was not afraid of the man-scent which once was horrid in his nostrils. Suddenly Saya's face took on the determined look it had worn so often in the past few days. He ran to his waiting mount and took from the saddle a bladder of a sheep which was filled with water. Quickly he tore a strip from his burnoose and then quietly he walked to the horse. Speaking softly he began to cleanse the wound in the animal's side.

"So grey one, you do not scream in rage at me. Perhaps you know I love you, eh? Softly I move near you, and you must be careful too. I am only a boy, grey one. If your great hoof should strike me it would kill me. Quiet, wild one. See . . . I am your friend. You bleed badly, my beautiful horse, and when you struggle to rise it is worse. Quietly, quietly, quietly. . . ."

And thus murmuring aimlessly but softly to the horse, Saya cleansed the ugly wound. The stallion quieted, partly from the soothing voice of the boy, partly because the great loss of blood drained the strength from his powerful body.

Then the bleeding began to slow. The cooling water cleansed the wound and Saya was able to work with greater ease. The little desert boy, brought up with horses, knew them as another boy might know his arithmetic. With the stallion quiet, he even dared explore the wound. Suddenly he straightened up and joy came into his eyes again! For his fingers held a smashed and flattened bullet.

"Grey one!" he cried. "Grey one! The bullet! A rib stopped its course. You are not badly hurt! Only the bleeding is bad. Grey one, you will live! You will live and I will help you to live!"

Saya now fell to work with a vengeance. Again and again the cleansing cloth worked over the wound. Khala Hawa for the most part lay quietly on the sand, apparently enjoying the ministering hands of the boy. Though now and again, despite the fact that Saya's hands were as gentle as a woman's, the sharp pain would bring the stallion's head up and he would nicker a pointed warning. Once a shining black hoof struck swiftly at the boy as the powerful body of the horse tensed with the hurt. As the hoof flashed past, barely missing him, Saya put down the cloth. Resting his hands on the tender bridge of the horse's silken nose, he spoke softly but firmly. The stallion tried to draw in his head, to bring it close to his chest and thus escape the boy's strong hands. Now the gentleness was gone and the pressure on his sensitive nose suddenly told Khala Hawa that this strange man-thing, besides his comforting gentleness, had also a way of force which was hard to understand. For a horse, even the wisest, has not the intelligence of a dog, and he must be taught not only by kindness but firmness also.

The struggle was unequal. Khala Hawa was sorely weakened by his great loss of blood and though he threshed and tried to rise, the strong brown fingers continued their pressure, until finally the great stallion lay quietly in the sand, completely exhausted by his own struggles.

But now Saya's hands dropped away from the tender nose and, for a moment, stroked the silky ears and the shining grey of the horse's powerful neck. Now again the cool hands, and the cooler water applied themselves to the wound. And Khala Hawa found it good, for his hurt had begun to throb mightily. But the bleeding had stopped and Saya wet the cloth well, folded it and placed it carefully into the wound to ease the pain.

As he finished, the desert night was suddenly upon them. Where a short moment before the sun shone brightly, the darkness was falling almost as rapidly as though a curtain were drawn over the sky. The desert night is cold and now, in the chill of the darkness, Saya drew his burnoose tightly about him, and wondered if there were not some way to shield the great stallion against the cold. But the sand of the desert floor on which Khala Hawa lay was warm with the heat of the earlier desert sun, held there by his own body. The great horse with his pain eased, his nervousness quieted by Saya, fell asleep.

Saya smiled and rose to find the horse he had ridden from camp. Then he stopped, for a moment, stunned. The mare was gone and there remained only her tracks in the sand as, unattended, she had turned and followed the other horses home. Saya straightened anxiously trying to see through the darkness. He listened carefully but the death-like silence of the desert gave up no drumming of hooves. Then, shrugging as though being stranded on the desert with a wounded horse was an everyday occurrence, Saya lay down on the sand and stretched out, snuggling close to Khala Hawa's muscular back. Warmed by the sand and the heat of the stallion's great body, Saya dropped off quickly to sleep. One of the boy's arms rose and fell across the broad chest of the horse. As the arm went across him Khala Hawa was awake in an instant: his head came up. The great neck thrust backward and the wide-set nostrils flared as the stallion bared his teeth. Then the horse caught the newfound scent of the strange man-thing. His own scent lay heavily on the brown hand of the boy. The soft muzzle closed over the shining white teeth and, with a nicker the stallion dropped his head back to the warm sand. His eyes closed and again he slept. One by one the stars came out to stream their light down upon the horse and the boy, and perhaps they wondered at these strange bedfellows.

Saya was awakened at the first glimmering of dawn, and rather forcefully. In fact, he was tumbled about in the sand when Khala Hawa gathered his legs underneath his powerful body and, as horses do, lunged to his feet. Recovering quickly, Saya arose to his feet.

Shaking the sand from his burnoose, he looked at the great grey horse. Now again did the big stallion feel the fear of the man-thing. Arching his neck, he snorted loudly and pawed the ground with one shining hoof. He seemed poised to wheel in flight when Saya smiled, extended his hand and spoke to him:

"So my great horse," he said. "You did not fly in the night then? I thought you would not. Come now. Come to Saya."

So saying, the boy walked slowly toward the grey horse, his hand still extended. Khala Hawa pranced with his forefeet, snorted and puffed and once lifted his head to send the mighty scream of the stallion ringing across the desert. But something stayed the wild horse. The terrible weakness was still with his body. The scent of the kindly, strong brown hands, perhaps reminded the horse of the still throbbing wound in his side. At any rate, all these things helped to dominate the simple instinct which directs a horse. As the hand of Saya reached out to caress the silky muzzle and then to slide up and scratch the forehead between the eyes, the horse dropped all pretense of anger and, lowering his head, stood quietly.

Then Saya walked around to examine the horse's wound. Khala Hawa flinched as the boy touched the tender place, but made no protest. What Saya saw pleased him. The wound was already drying, the first sign of healing. Saya looked anxiously at the great horse even though he was pleased at the progress of the wound. Well he knew that the fine animal had lost considerable blood, and though he seemed at the peak of his power, his considerable weakness would soon sap the small strength gained in the night's rest. Yet . . . they must move, and at once, for the desert held only death. Saya had no rope nor could he devise one with which to lead the horse. And if he had a rope, Khala Hawa would only have been frightened of it. With the confidence of one who has a great knowledge of horses, the boy reached up and took a firm grip upon the forelock of the stallion. Then he spoke again to Khala Hawa.

"Now we will go my horse, and you come with me. Do not be frightened for I mean to you only the greatest of good. Come."

Taken completely by surprise, the powerful horse stepped forward without hesitation at the tug on his forelock and together they started their terrible march across the desert, the sands of which though cool from that night, would soon be a roaring furnace.

On and on they moved, the hooves of the horse and the feet of the boy making little wakes in the loose surface sand, such as might be made by tiny boats in the water. But the ever-present desert wind would smooth out the marks of their passing and again shape the sand into rippling rows. Just as their footprints slowly disappeared, so did the prints of the horses of

Akim Abou and his men fade. Soon Saya found that he was following a trackless way and, without the hoofprints to follow, he was forced to stop and take his bearings again and again. Saya was not lost. The desert was to him no more than a great sea of sand to be crossed at will. But always before in crossing the desert Saya had been mounted on a swift horse or camel. Now, plodding slowly through the sand the burning sun struck through his burnoose. Soon his head began to ache dully and his legs became heavy things to drag, one after the other, now this one, now that one, until he felt that he could no longer move.

Again and again however, he would pause to run his hand over the silken nose of Khala Hawa and several times through blurred, red-rimmed eyes he looked carefully at the bullet wound in the grey horse's side. Even in his parched agony Saya could see that the wound was well dried and that the splendid health of the big horse would soon see it healed. But it was not the wound which was bothering Khala Hawa. The great quantity of blood he had lost on the desert sand was too much for even his muscular frame to withstand. Slowly the power drained from his body. More and more the shining black hooves dragged in the sand, his great head dropped lower and lower as his need for water grew. Saya did not realize it but his own steps slowed with the steps of the horse until, almost as though by agreement, they took one last step and stopped atop a sand dune. For several minutes they stood, both too fatigued to move, heads bowed, dully unaware of anything but heat and thirst and pain. Thus they stood for several minutes until finally strength left the boy's fingers. Releasing his hold on the horse's mane he slid in a crumpled heap at Khala Hawa's feet.

The great horse looked with glazed eyes at the boy who seemed oddly enough to have become part of himself. Then overcome by his own fatigue, he sank down on the sand to rest. How long they lay there Saya never knew, though it must have been mid-afternoon when he struggled to consciousness. His benumbed brain told him only one thing. In his delirium, induced by the terrible beating heat and fatigue, Saya was again attending the wounded Khala Hawa. On hands and knees he crawled to the side of the horse. Realizing dimly that the wound was on the other side he tried to climb over the back of the prostrate stallion. The effort was too great and again blessed unconsciousness relieved his pain. Astraddle the sturdy back of the grey horse Saya sank into oblivion.

Perhaps it was the light weight of the boy on his back which caused Khala Hawa to raise his head, but raise it he did just as a change in the vagrant breeze brought a familiar scent to his nostrils. Now his fine, close-set ears pricked up. He essayed a weak snort and slowly scrambled to his feet. Even in his coma, Saya clung to the stallion's back as the grey horse lunged across the desert, clumsy in his weakness. Khala Hawa, wild, fierce stallion of the desert, king of the land of sand, raider of horse herds was carrying a rider! On and on the great horse went, moving not alone by muscular power, but by the tremendous will born of the wild animal's instinct to survive. For what Khala Hawa had smelled on the breeze was water . . . cool, life-giving water!

It was a cruel hour which finally brought them to the tiny oasis in mid-desert. The lunging steps of the stallion brought Saya back to consciousness, but so weak was the boy, so tortured . . . his tongue swollen and protruding from his lips . . . that he hardly knew or cared that he bestrode his beloved horse. Straight into the little oasis between the tall date palms went Khala Hawa to the tiny spring which formed a small, crystal-clear pool in the rocks from which it came. Gratefully the grey horse dropped to his knees and buried his muzzle in the water. Saya slid from his back and, crawling to the little pool, buried his own face in the water so close that his tan cheek brushed the grey cheek of the stallion. Refreshed, boy and horse again lay side by side in the sand to sleep for many hours.

Saya awoke at mid-morning to find Khala Hawa a short distance away grazing on the lush green which grew all about them. Again the desert blazed with sun-fire and shimmering heat-waves danced until one's eyes grew weary with the strange movements. In the little oasis the air was cooled by the lightest of breezes. Now Saya realized that he too was hungry. He rose to his feet, and extended his hand to the grey horse who raised his head to watch. This time Khala Hawa came quickly forward and placed his head in Saya's hands to be caressed, for now they were united in a bond which could never be broken. Each had given life back to the other and now the boy and the great horse shared the full love which sometimes exists between a man and an animal. Khala Hawa did not know it, but he had been conquered by pain, and won by loving care.

But now there was much to be done. Two empty bellies demanded filling and with a last pat on his horse's silky nose, Saya turned to climb a date palm for the luscious fruit he could see hanging in high clusters. Khala Hawa eagerly returned to the heavy green grass. All that day they rested and ate and drank the cool, sweet water. Again that night they slept side by side. The next day, arising in the cool of the morning, Saya felt that his strength had returned. As for Khala Hawa, he walked to his grazing place for his morning meal in high spirits. Despite the still sore wound in his side, he could not resist kicking up his heels and bucking playfully, though a sharp twinge made him desist more quickly than he had started. Saya laughed happily, and almost for the first time in days, spoke:

"So-ho, my great grey one! The strength is returning and with it comes the spirit, eh?"

Khala Hawa stopped in his tracks and looked round at the boy. Then, turning, he trotted quickly back and thrust his head into the boy's hand, for, not understanding the words, he took the sound of Saya's voice for an invitation to have his ears scratched. Saya laughed again, and understanding what was in the mind of the stallion he did scratch the tiny ears, before sending the animal back to his grazing with a gentle push.

After a quick breakfast of dates, Saya set to work. Now there was a job to be done, and Saya knew exactly how to do it. Vaguely in his mind was the memory of his ride on Khala Hawa's back, and while the remembrance of his own pain and suffering was fast fading, he recalled with a thrill the long, free-swinging gait which was apparent even then in the lunging walk of the near-to-death horse. Saya tore a wide strip from his burnoose and this he carefully tore into narrower strips. Now, braiding the strips, he carefully fashioned a light, but fairly strong bridle and reins. Not having a bit, Saya fashioned one of cloth, fastening to it the reins which, when pulled upon, would tighten the loop on the lower jaw of the horse. True, both bridle and reins, though braided and stronger for that, were made of cloth. Khala Hawa could have snapped them with a thrust of his powerful neck. But that was no matter. Not even the heaviest of leather bridles and reins could hold Khala Hawa if he so willed. Saya knew the great stallion must be ruled by firmness tempered with love, and not by force. Saya also knew, and wisely so, that the strongest man is a weakling compared to the weakest horse. If Khala Hawa was ever to submit to a rider and a master, the cloth bridle and reins would serve as well as anything else.

He let Khala Hawa eat his fill. Then as the stallion began to look out over the desert and send his ringing screams reverberating from one sand dune to another, Saya approached him.

"So my great grey one," he said. "Now must come your first lesson. See what I have."

The boy held up the bridle and reins and Khala Hawa examined them carefully with his great flaring nostrils. Then he lost interest. It smelled exactly like the boy he was growing to love—so everything must be all right. However, Saya's brown hand lay on the tender bridge of the horse's nose and, as Khala Hawa was about to turn away, the wiry fingers closed for a moment. Khala Hawa's attention was recaptured at once. As the stallion looked at the boy in some surprise, Saya took the opportunity to slip the bridle over his head. Letting the reins hang to the ground Saya stepped back to watch the reaction. The grey stallion snorted at the strange white strips hanging from his nose, bobbed his head which made the strips jump, which in turn, made him jump. But before fear and panic took hold of the stallion the laughter and soft voice of the boy quieted him. Again he thrust his great head into the lad's hands for the cloth tickled and now his nose needed scratching again. Saya understood and took pains to scratch the places where the cloth bridle lay, because in so doing, he was able to move the bridle about and thus accustom the horse to its feel. Contented, Khala Hawa offered no objection when, holding the reins in one hand, and the forelock of the horse in the other Saya walked slowly forward as he had when they started their nearly fatal trek across the desert. Gradually the boy's hold on the forelock was loosened and slowly he moved in front of the horse until finally Saya had only to pick up the reins and Khala Hawa followed willingly.

The great horse learned many things that day and in the days that followed. He learned to let Saya pick up each of his feet and with a sharp stick clean away the sand from the "v" of the frog in the center of the hoof. He learned quickly to kneel in the sand, for to the desert man this is important. In the desert, a black cloud will suddenly appear on the horizon, then a wind blows up which grows stronger and stronger. Any Arab on the desert will watch these manifestations closely waiting for the sudden shouted command of the leader: "Kneel your horses." Then, quickly ordering their horses down, they cover both the horses' heads and their own with their burnooses, thus protecting themselves until the sandstorm, scourge of the desert, has blown itself out. 1431069

Saya waited until the fourth day to mount Khala Hawa. But now he knew that he must finish his job quickly. The wound in the horse's side was healing rapidly, and while he had established a closeness with the wild horse, still he knew that Khala Hawa was not one to spend his days in idleness. Saya knew that now he must establish his mastery over the stallion. He slipped the bridle on the sleek grey head, and the horse barely paused in its grazing, so accustomed had it become to the strange appliance. Now, taking up the reins, Saya put Khala Hawa through each of the points in training which the horse had thus far received. Tossing the reins over the horse's head, Saya suddenly leaped astride the muscular back. At once he began to speak in soothing tones to the big grey horse. But Khala Hawa was still a wild horse, and this was too much. Suddenly and mysteriously his beloved companion was gone, and though he could still hear the familiar voice, the horse was much more concerned with the weight suddenly dropped upon his back. Though a horse's eyes are so placed that he can look backward or forward, Khala Hawa's fright was such that he could not recognize the weight on his back as Saya. Accordingly, as his panic grew, he suddenly arched his back and lunged high in the air, bucking and plunging and bending his powerful body into every shape. But Saya was ready. He dropped the useless cloth reins and clinging to the heavy mane, he clamped his legs firmly and tightly about the heaving sides of the stallion.

There are some riders who seem to be almost grown to the horse's back, so well do they sit their mounts, regardless of how the horse misbehaves. Saya was one of these.

Again and again the great stallion leaped high in the air, turning and twisting, to strike the earth with stunning force. And each time, it was a shock to Saya's body almost as brutal as the blow of a club. The boy's head was snapped back and forth so often that he thought it would detach itself from his neck and roll across the sand. But he clung tightly to Khala Hawa's back, knowing full well that if he did not win this first contest, he would never have another chance. A thin trickle of blood appeared, flowing from the nostrils of the boy, and his arms became leaden weights. All feeling went out of the legs, clamped so tightly to the great barrel which was Khala Hawa's chest. A murmured prayer to Allah escaped the boy's lips, and he was about to release his rapidly weakening hold and give up the unequal struggle when the wild horse suddenly changed his tactics. To Khala

Hawa's mind came the decision that if he could not fling this clinging, frightening weight from his back, he could run away from it. As his shining black hooves struck the ground from one last wild plunge, they as quickly spurned it, and Khala Hawa set out across the desert in a wild run.

To an expert horseman the full gallop of a horse is as easy to sit as the gentle swing of a rocking chair, for of all the gaits, the gallop is the smoothest. Now Saya could relax his grim hold, and sitting erect, he passed his hand wearily over his blood smeared face, and wiped the sweat from his smarting eyes. Though his body throbbed with pain, a tired but happy smile

crossed the boy's face, and the wild yell of the desert Arab winged across the sands. Saya was happy now. He was riding faster than any man had ever ridden before, and with heel and voice, he urged the great horse to an even faster pace, for Saya knew that now, and only now, could he establish the mastery over the stallion which was so necessary if the horse were ever to be fully tamed.

But now, outraged nature began to assert herself. Khala Hawa's wound, which was only beginning to heal, broke open, and with the trickling blood came also a sharp, stabbing pain at each movement. His body, already much diminished in strength from the wound, was now drained entirely. He was not even aware that Saya had picked up the light cloth reins, and with a gentle pressure kept his sleek head turned slightly, thus causing him to work his way in a great circle, until as his steps slowed to a tired walk, they were already approaching the oasis. Now Saya spoke to him, gently and soothingly.

"So my great one, it was good to run again with the swiftness of the wind, eh? That is why I have named you Wind of the Desert . . . Khala Hawa. But now you tire, and see, again your wound bleeds and brings you pain. So my dear one, all this must be and more, though it grieves me to bring you hurt. Many lessons must you learn so that you may live a long and happy life with me, and not again be hunted, perhaps next time to die. So now my good horse . . . slow, slow, slow."

The gentle pressure of the tightening loop about the stallion's lower jaw as Saya drew on the reins, and the soothing tones of the boy's voice finally had their effect. Khala Hawa faltered and stopped at the edge of the tiny desert haven. Saya slid from his back and limped forward to take the sweat-blackened head of the stallion in his hands.

"So my sweet one when the breath comes back to your body we will go. Think not of me as a cruel one. Only do I know that what must be done, must be done now."

Saya worked rapidly, or rather, as rapidly as his wracked and tired body would let him. He made a bundle of dates, and filled the sheep-bladder again with the sweet water from the spring. By now the great lungs of Khala Hawa were quiet, and the stallion stood wearily, head down, almost completely exhausted from his struggles. But Saya knew that there was reserve strength in that great body, and he was counting on this, plus the fact that weariness would make the wild horse tractable. For Saya had determined to bring the horse to the home camp when, with the proper equipment, and the help of the great horsemen among his father's men, he could properly finish the taming and training of the wild horse. Saya knew that the surging wild spirit of the great grey stallion would never be broken, nor did he want that, but the boy, wise in the ways of horses knew also that they are creatures of habit, and once a habit is established, it remains with the animal forever.

Now Saya, his bundle of dates and his skin of water fastened securely to his back, walked to the drooping horse. He spoke soothingly to the stallion, who lifted his head to sniff briefly at the boy's body, only to drop it wearily again as though the effort were far too great to make. Though his own body was throbbing with aches, Saya managed to vault to Khala Hawa's back. The startled horse raised his head quickly, and his body tensed. Again the soothing voice of the boy reassured him, and he quieted. For the moment, all fight was gone from the big grey horse, and he wanted only to rest. But Saya lifted the reins and, touching the horse firmly in the sides with his heels, the boy shifted his weight far forward on the high withers. Instantly, as his delicate sense of balance was disturbed, Khala Hawa moved forward to regain it, and without volition, was soon moving, though slowly, across the desert toward the camp of Akim Abou.

Again an exhausted boy and horse moved across the desert sands. And while this time the boy rode upon the powerful back, his bruised and battered body cried for relief as each jolting step of the weary horse sent stabs of pain into every aching muscle.

But Saya set his teeth, and held to his resolve. Though the horse now accepted him, and even showed some measure of affection, hard-won by the boy's ministrations, he was still a wild thing, and far from ready to accept life with men. Cruel though it might seem, Saya continued to urge the stallion on, and, his senses dulled with fatigue, Khala Hawa continued his shuffling way through the desert sand. Saya's heart ached for his beloved mount, but he consoled himself that he was taking the horse to a new life, a life which would be happier, safer and far longer.

Two days, with only enough rest to keep them from dying from exhaustion, finally brought them to the camp of Akim Abou. It was with his last bit of strength that Saya fashioned a hobble for the forelegs of the big stallion so that he could not stray into the desert to be lost forever among the dunes. Then the boy sought his father's tent, where he fell into his sleeping robes to sleep away a day and a night.

As for Khala Hawa he stood with bowed head for a time, then his forelegs buckled slowly and he let his weary body sink to the warm sand. Not even the strong scent of many men frightened him, nor was he disturbed when the other horses moved close to observe this new one. His eyes closed and he slept. Though he did not know it, Khala Hawa had already begun to accept this new life; a life which would be made full with love and kindness, exciting with strange and sometimes fearful happenings, but with all, a comfortable life with a plentitude of food, and a full measure of safety. Life was not ending for Khala Hawa. Indeed it was only beginning.

Chapter 3

THE TENT OF Akim Abou was quiet, though outside, the camp was a-bustle with activity as usual. The sheik himself sat at one side of the entrance, sipping coffee and puffing at his water-pipe. Occasionally his eyes wandered to the dark pile of robes in the corner which concealed his sleeping son, and his eyes twinkled. Corza, his lovely wife, moved nervously about the tent, tending the pots of food which she kept warm over a small fire of camel-dung. When her eyes fell upon the sleeping Saya, they grew tender, but a little worried frown about her mouth testified to her anxiety for the sleeping boy.

Saya came awake slowly. Then at the sudden remembrance of the wild stallion, hobbled and left with the horse herd, he flung aside the robes to bound erect. But his stiffened muscles screamed a tortured warning and he sank back upon the robes. At once his mother was at his side.

"Saya," she said. "Lie down again. Rest long and well my son."

But Saya shook his head and, more slowly this time, rose from the pile of robes and cautiously stretched his aching arms and legs. Akim Abou lightly caressed his beard which was hiding an amused smile. But there was a note of pride in his voice when he spoke:

"The boy cannot lie longer in the robes, wife. He has work to do."

Corza protested swiftly.

"But my husband, the boy is tired to his death. He is hurt and nearly sick with weariness."

Akim Abou lifted his hand for silence.

"Though this be true," he said firmly. "It is also true that he has brought among us our old enemy, the wild stallion. Having done this, it is for Saya to protect the camp from the animal."

Saya's eyes grew round at this new thought and he realized for the first time the damage Khala Hawa could cause should he so desire. He turned to his father.

"But my father, the horse is no longer a wild animal." Now, quickly Saya told his father all that had happened, his treatment of the wound, the wild ride when he "broke" the horse and the subsequent trip to the home camp. Akim Abou did not interrupt, though he occasionally nodded his head, and the burbling of his water-pipe betrayed the inner excitement which he was at pains to conceal from his son. When Saya finished, he spoke.

"You have accomplished much, my son, and perhaps it is not for me to council you now. This wild one is the horse of your heart, and Allah has placed him in your hands. So be it. Now the task is yours. But this I will say. The horse may be likened to a man. Each man must learn to live with his neighbors in peace and happiness and goodness. If he does not, if he trespasses against his neighbor, then he is made to become an outcast. So it is with the horse. If you can draw from his soul the wildness and bring him to love and obey you, he will be welcomed by all the men and the beasts in our camp. If you cannot. . . ."

Akim Abou shrugged, and lifted his hands to let them fall expressively. But Saya's eyes were shining and he answered quickly.

"He will love me father, I am sure. But much more must I do. I must teach him many things."

Akim Abou nodded. He was aware that his son already possessed much wisdom, and that no man was more skilled with horses. Akim Abou was content, and so he spoke a final word.

"We learn life through pain and happiness. So must your horse. We are punished for wrong doing, rewarded for good. So also with your horse. Remember this my son. A small pain to your horse today may save him a great hurt tomorrow."

It was thus that Saya began the training of Khala Hawa. Saya was a good trainer, for he had the patience of the desert man who feels that time is his servant, not his master. As the weeks went by Khala Hawa learned many things. Saya worked hard. He gave the stallion no time to brood over the restraints placed upon him. The horse learned quickly that Saya was the source of many good things. Regular nourishing food filled out the gaunt places in Khala Hawa's powerful body. Brushing soon smoothed out the raggedness in the beautiful grey coat. The wild thing's fear of man faded slowly until, indeed, the horse was unaware of its passing. Though at first when Saya mounted him for his daily lesson the big horse pitched and bucked, these wild gyrations grew fewer and fewer, until finally Saya could vault to his back from either side, and the stallion stood quietly until Saya's signal sent him forward.

It was a proud day when Saya rode Khala Hawa through the camp for the first time, to stop at his father's tent. The beautiful animal stood quietly, his head high, neck arched, and tiny ears pointed forward as he watched the boy who dismounted to stand at his head, reins in hand. Now as the people of the camp crowded around to admire and praise, the long weeks of patient work with the big stallion were rewarded. No fear showed in the great eyes, nor did the horse flinch at the touch of strange hands. Instead he eagerly watched the boy, for Khala Hawa had learned that life with Saya was good in many ways. The saddle resting lightly on his withers, the tasselled bridle on his head told the great horse that soon he would be racing across the sand, enjoying to the fullest the wind singing in his ears, and the sand pluming out behind his flying hooves.

The crowd dissolved finally, each person going about his duties. Saya turned to mount for his ride when a welcome voice called his name, and he turned back happily to greet his little sister. Nedda's big brown eyes sparkled with excitement.

"Saya," she cried. "You have brought Khala Hawa into the camp! Was he frightened?"

Perhaps Saya's answering smile was a little superior, but his pride in his fine horse was pardonable.

"Frightened? My Khala Hawa is a lion among horses. He is afraid of nothing."

Nedda nodded.

"You have worked hard and well, Saya. Do you ride today?"

Saya nodded, then looked thoughtfully at his sister. "I have not yet taken a long trip with the horse. I should do this."

Nedda waited for she knew Saya was not finished.

"Nedda," he said. "Come close to Khala Hawa. Come."

Nedda did as she was bidden, stepping close to the great horse's head. Now Saya turned to Khala Hawa, and his slim hands moved over the smooth hide and patted the sleek neck.

"So my big one. Here is another you must learn to love. This is Nedda."

Nedda put her tiny hand out to the great horse's muzzle. He nuzzled it gently and smelled it carefully. Intermingled with the strange scent of the girl was the familiar scent of his beloved new master. Khala Hawa accepted Nedda. Saya looked at Nedda with a sparkle in his eye.

"Nedda do you remember a time ago when father set up camp for one night at Jedda oasis?"

Nedda nodded happily. "Yes Saya I remember well, for there the dates were huge and the best I ever tasted."

"That is what I mean," Saya answered. "Nedda, let us go there and eat some of those dates!"

Nedda was amazed. "Today? You and I? But Jedda oasis is a day's ride. I know because we used a full day to come here."

Saya smiled. "I can see that even you do not understand my horse. Khala Hawa will carry us there and back. And we will be home in time for the evening meal. Come, my sister. It will be an adventure. Khala Hawa! Stand! Now, Nedda, up you go for a ride like the wind of the desert."

Jedda oasis was in bloom. The sweet water spring which gushed from between two huge rocks made a paradise of this tiny spot in the desert. The date palms grew high and rich clusters of the fragrant fruit hung ready for the picker's hand. From far across the sand the great grey horse smelled the green and the water of Jedda and he whinnied happily for this had been a favorite spot when he ran wild and free across the desert before the bullet of Emal Dukka brought him down.

Hardly noticing the light weight of Saya and Nedda he ran with breathtaking speed, needing no urging. This, after all, was a fine life for a great horse. Carrying a beloved little master to a lovely place where choice food to eat and delicious water to drink were waiting. Khala Hawa was happy. And Saya and Nedda were happier than they had ever been. Saya was astride the horse he had longed to own, being carried swifter than man had ever ridden before, and that made him happy. Nedda was happy because her brother was happy, and because of the swift ride, and the prospect of delicious dates.

And so they rode into Jedda oasis. Saya guided Khala Hawa to the spring and the three of them drank their fill. Then, while the grey stallion grazed on the tender green shrubs and grasses, Saya and Nedda, agile as two monkeys, climbed the tall palms and gathered clusters of ripe dates. After they had eaten their fill they played among the high trees and in the tall grasses that grew near the spring. Khala Hawa grazed farther and farther from them, finally reaching the edge of the oasis, where the desert sand thinned out the grasses and then stretched away to disappear behind the far horizon.

Tired of their play Saya and Nedda curled up in the shade of a low spreading palm for a nap. Khala Hawa filled with tender shrubs and his thirst quenched with sweet water trotted out on the desert as habit had taught him to do through hundreds of visits to Jedda oasis.

From far out on the desert there came to his ears the voices of wild horses and the scent of a beautiful wild mare who had long been in his desert herd. Not one of the three suspected the approaching danger which was even now moving across the hot sand toward Jedda. A caravan, winding in and out among the dunes like a long, many-legged worm, made slow but steady progress. Camels plodded patiently but tirelessly, and some men rode beside the line on fine Arab and Berber horses. But most of the caravan was a pitiful sight to see, for it was composed of men, women and children, and they were chained together in a long, unbreakable line.

No slavers were more vicious than the two men who headed the caravan now approaching Jedda oasis. Kooba and Hassan knew their dangerous and vile profession better than most. Each of them was ready with gun, sword, dagger or whip to enforce his will. And these were the two who dismounted from the horses and stood over the sleeping children.

Kooba spoke with pleasure: "See Hassan. Here in Jedda we find food and water and two more slaves, eh? I know a certain sultan who will pay a fancy price for house servants as young and strong as these."

Hassan grinned evilly through his black wiry beard. "It is as you say, Kooba. Shall we take them to the end of the line and put the chains on them?"

Kooba considered for a moment.

"It is not needed now. Let us eat our food and rest. We can chain them as the caravan moves past here in the morning. Meanwhile, wake them and tie them to a tree, eh?"

Hassan relished his job, for he was as cruel as he was evil. Roughly he shook the two children awake and flung them against a tree and tied them. Saya's anger flamed once when Hassan twisted his little sister's arm and made her cry out in pain. He doubled his small fists and beat the big man. But Hassan roughly flung him aside.

"Let her alone," Saya cried. "Let my sister alone!"

A hard slap knocked him to the ground and dazed him. When his head cleared from the cowardly blow he and Nedda were both securely tied to a date palm. Hassan grinned at them again and spoke:

"Save your strength," he said. "Slaves have hard work to do." And he turned on his heel and walked away from them to a fire where a mutton was roasting.

"Slaves!" Then this was a slaving caravan. To Saya and Nedda slavers were nothing new, but something to be feared. How often had they run to the protection of the women as their father and his men snatched up their long rifles and hurried to fight off a raiding party. Saya wasted no time in tears. Quickly he worked at the ropes which tied him and Nedda to the tree, meanwhile quieting his sister who was badly frightened. Saya's hands were strong, and even better he was supple of finger and wrist. Working swiftly, his hands writhed in the loops of rope like two brown snakes, he felt a sudden loosening of the tension. His right hand was free. Carefully he worked at the ropes. As his hands freed, the ropes went slack about them, and Saya was quick to draw them snug again so their escape should not be noticed. However, with the knots thus loosened, Nedda's tiny hands slipped easily out of the bonds. Saya cautioned her to hold the ropes in her hands behind her so that the slack would not give their escape away. Now Saya lifted his head, and sent a ringing call out over the desert!

"Khala Hawa! Come! Come quickly!"

Kooba the slaver lifted his head from the robe on which he was resting.

"Quiet you," he demanded. "Or I will wring your neck!" Then he lay back again on his robe.

Khala Hawa moved rapidly across the desert sands. So high was his action that his gleaming hooves seemed hardly to touch the sand. Then from far beyond the dunes came the neighing of a mare. He recognized the sound and his head lifted high. Back across the sand he sent an answering call and his great stride lengthened to the floating gallop which Saya knew so well. Straight as an arrow might travel Khala Hawa went, clearing small dunes in tremendous leaps, bounding up and down the high dunes as though they were level ground.

It was on the crest of a high dune that Saya's voice faintly reached his ear. In the desert the clear air and absence of obstruction permit sound to travel far. Faintly the boy's voice struck the sensitive ear of the great stallion and brought him to that plunging halt which no other horse could equal. And then again came the call of the mare. Khala Hawa whinnied unhappily torn between the two voices. He trotted slowly in the direction of the mare's voice, then he trotted back toward the oasis. Then he stopped and listened, ears erect, body rigid as a statue! But no further call came from Saya, and suddenly as though he had made up his mind he plunged at full gallop down the side of the dune in the direction from which the mare had given voice.

But no! The love of Saya and his love for the boy were strong in his mind. Khala Hawa was still a horse, and once trained properly a horse never forgets the training! Khala Hawa had been trained and well to respond instantly to Saya's voice, and now he seemed to feel the boy's gentle hands on his nose and neck, the same slim fingers which eased the pain of his terrible wound. Now at a thundering gallop he drove in a great circle; head high, powerful legs thrusting the sand behind him as though it were to be spurned, he bore down on Jedda oasis with the speed of an approaching sandstorm.

Khala Hawa did not know it but in that moment he had lost the last of his wildness. Never again would the desert know him as a free, wild spirit. From now on he would follow Saya until his great heart stilled.

Not knowing that his call was heard Saya stood as he had been tied and Nedda stood quietly with him. Nedda was quiet because she was miserable and unhappy, but Saya stood listening carefully. Soon he heard that for which he listened, the drumming of great hoofs far out over the sand, coming nearer and nearer. The fast, unbroken rhythm could only be his great stallion, Khala Hawa! And then over a sand dune flashed the shining body of the great grey horse. Khala Hawa was running as he had never run. In his nostrils was a hated man-scent, an evil scent it seemed to the horse, for some unknown sense seemed to warn him of danger, and it was to this place Saya had called him! When Saya saw him he could restrain himself no longer!

"Khala Hawa," he cried. "Hurry grey one, hurry!"

Now Saya flung away the ropes which no longer held them, and grasping Nedda's hand, he half dragged the little girl over the rough ground toward the oncoming horse. When he saw them, Khala Hawa lifted his head and voiced the shrill, terrifying scream of the wild stallion. Kooba, awakened, jumped from his robes, saw the stallion running to meet his two new slaves, who themselves were loose and racing for their freedom.

With a curse he kicked the sleeping Hassan awake, and turned to shout for his guards. But he and Hassan had carefully set up their tent well away from the noisy caravan of slaves, and the guards were at a distance where his shout went unnoticed. Now, snatching up a heavy cane, Kooba set out in pursuit of the children, followed by the half-asleep Hassan. But it was useless. Already Saya and Nedda had reached the side of Khala Hawa, who stood at command until they could mount. With a cry, Kooba raised the heavy cane in fury, and flung it straight at the little group. It struck Saya between the shoulders and the boy, his breath taken away, fell to the ground. Looba leaped toward them with Hassan at his heels, but the men did not reckon with Khala Hawa. Well did the big horse recognize the movement of the thrown cane, for often when he was a wild colt a thrown stone or stick had bruised his tender hide. And now the two men were leaping straight for him, and they could only be enemies.

His small ears laid back against his head, his neck arched like a striking snake, and fire flamed in his eyes. With a tremendous leap he flung himself, a half ton of furious muscle, at the oncoming men. Looba saw the great horse bearing down on him and turned to run, only to go headlong into Hassan who came running up behind him, spilling them both to the ground. Before they could rise the flashing forehoofs came down once, twice, and it was all over. Hassan and Kooba lay still on the ground, blood streaming from their terrible wounds. Nedda, hands over her eyes to cover the frightening sight, permitted a little scream to escape her lips, but it was enough to bring Saya fully back to his senses. And it was well timed, for the disturbance finally reached the ears of the guards, and they were beginning to seek the source of the commotion.

Rising from the ground Saya helped Nedda to her feet and they ran to the side of the stallion who waited quietly. The guards of the caravan, uncertain as to what had happened, snatched up their rifles and looked about wildly for a target. A few shots were fired, and the bullets whined around them like angry bees. Khala Hawa disregarded the bullets. Saya helped Nedda to the horse's back, and jumped up himself, then bending low over the stallion's neck, he paused for one quick caress, then cried:

"Go Khala Hawa! Run so that even the bullets fall behind!"

With a great bound the magnificent horse plunged forward. Now the caravan guards, grouped together in their puzzlement were directly before him. Straight at them he ran, and coming among them he bowled them over like tenpins, and then the mighty stallion straightened out in the floating gallop which was one day to make him the most famous horse in Arabia!

Straight for the tents of Akim Abou's camp he went, and at a speed that, as Saya had promised, would bring them home in time for the evening meal.

Chapter 4

THE PASSAGE OF Khala Hawa through the little group of guards scattered them as a hurricane would scatter a pile of dried leaves. Some of them were flung to the ground with sufficient force to render them unconscious. Others, slashed by the flying hooves of the great horse, moaned in pain, their weapons lying forgotten in the sand. The few left standing looked around in bewilderment at this sudden turn of events.

Then it was that Bunta, a giant negro wrote the last chapter in the history of this band of murderers. Bunta was a brave man and a wise one, and chief of his tribe of Zulus from Africa. The memory of the slavers' raid on his village still burned in his mind. Well he remembered how suddenly they descended on his village with rifles blazing. Outnumbered, Bunta and his warriors fought well and bravely, but their assagai, the spear of the African, and their bull-hide shields were no defense against bullets. Through the quick mind of Bunta passed the terrible picture of slaughter. He saw again the old men and women of his village chopped down ruthlessly, for the old ones were worthless as slaves. He saw the children and the young women put into chains, and those of the warriors who survived linked also into the long line to begin the march into bondage. And as Khala Hawa disappeared with Saya and Nedda over a sand dune at the edge of Jedda oasis, Bunta saw in the havoc wrought by the great horse the slaves' opportunity to regain their freedom. His great hands gathered in the chain which linked his arms, and leaping forward as far as the links which held him to the next in line would permit, he brought the shackles down on the head of a nearby guard who stood staring helplessly about him. Without a sound, the guard dropped to the ground to lie there inertly.

Then with a great shout Bunta called to his fellow captives to join him in his bid for freedom. Heads which had hung low during weeks of torturous marching, lifted. Eyes which had been dulled by the pain of torture brightened with a new hope. Into the minds of the slaves standing chained together, the picture of utter dejection, sprang a new resolve. Again their bodies smarted with the memory of the stinging whip lash, of thudding blows, or tortured hours marching under a blistering sun, weighed down with heavy chains, on this, the trail to the slave-block.

Suddenly they became aware of the words of Bunta, for he spoke in Swahili, a language all of them understood.

"Slaves! Follow me! Follow me to freedom!"

Then the thunder of two hundred voices rolled across the desert. Chained together as they were the slave line swept in a great arc as might the body of a gigantic snake, and encircled the cluster of guards. Heavy chains held in hands strong with the strength of desperation flailed. The guards of Hassan's and Kooba's caravan had at last met their match. Dazed by the rush of Khala Hawa and now overwhelmed by the sudden rebellion of slaves who by all rights should have lacked the strength and the courage for such an onslaught, the guards went down quickly. It must be related that the slaves showed no mercy, nor did the men of Hassan deserve it. Every man, woman and child in the long line of captives had seen at least one loved person die in the brutal raid on the villages. Not a guard was left alive.

It was Bunta who kept his head. His great voice

calling to them finally drove the madness from their brains, and they fell exhausted to the ground. It was Bunta who forced them to rise so that the line could shuffle forward to the body of Kooba who was the keeper of the keys which opened the great locks on the chains. Freeing himself quickly, Bunta went down the line quickly dropping the chains from the captives.

It was good that Bunta possessed many fine qualities of leadership. The slaves, suddenly freed from their terrible captivity began in their rage to destroy the camp. It was Bunta who finally brought them under control. Now from the supplies of the slavers he portioned out food to each person. Then each took a water skin and filled it from the sweet spring which had so recently quenched the thirsts of Nedda, Saya and Khala Hawa. Satisfied that the former slaves were provisioned for the long trek across the desert, Bunta sent them on their way with a wave of his great arm, then, following them he too disappeared into the trackless waste.

As the last of the slaves was swallowed by the ocean of sand, tiny black specks appeared high in the sky above Jedda oasis. Circling, circling the black specks dropped lower, until had there been anyone to look, they could have seen the great spread of wings, the ugly naked heads, the sharp cruel, curved beaks. The vultures were coming to the feast. The scavengers of the desert would finish the job and soon Jedda oasis, now a scene of carnage and violence, would be clean again, a beauty spot to offer rest and comfort to the weary desert traveller.

On the far side of Jedda oasis a hulking figure leaned on his long rifle and glanced disconsolately at the sun which was by now a blazing red ball, low in the sky and threatening momentarily to sink behind a far sand dune, and bring on the rush of darkness to enfold the desert. It was Kalim. Sent to the far side of the oasis as soon as the slave caravan arrived, for that approach must be guarded also, he knew nothing of the terrible battle which had freed the slaves. True he had heard the scattered shots which had been di-

rected at Khala Hawa, but shooting was nothing to worry oneself about, unless it was sustained. A few more dead slaves perhaps? It was not Kalim's concern. But now he was hungry. Long since, someone should have come to take his post and permit him to return to camp for his own evening meal. Knowing the tempers of Hassan and Kooba, however, he dared not leave his post to inquire into the delay, and so, hour after hour he had remained. Hunger gnawed at his belly, however, for Kalim was a huge man and much food was needed by his body. Finally his stomach's demands outweighed his fear of the slavers' wrath and with long determined steps he crossed the oasis and entered the camp.

Kalim stopped short at the sight and his shout of surprise sent the vultures flying with raucous squawks of protest. Quickly Kalim went from one guard to another. It was useless. What had been started by Khala Hawa and the slaves had been finished by the vultures. Only one body remained untouched by the great birds, and that was the body of Hassan. As Kalim approached, the reason was quickly apparent. Hassan stirred and moaned softly. He was still alive. It was the work of a moment for the hulking Kalim to heave Hassan to his shoulder and make his way to the spring. In due time under Kalim's clumsy ministrations, Hassan opened his eyes. When finally he could stand, he walked supported by Kalim to view the remains of the camp and the bodies of his dead henchmen. A terrible gash across his forehead testified to the sharp hoofs of Khala Hawa which had marked him forever, and the livid wound seemed to pulse with his rage at what he saw. He turned to Kalim and his hands clenched as he spoke.

"I will form a new band. I will gather men to me again. We will raid and raid and take many slaves. But first the boy of the Bedouin and the grey stallion will feel the revenge of Hassan!"

Chapter 5

THE LIFE OF the Bedouin is as wild as his world. He lives his nomadic life moving from place to place as his needs dictate facing countless dangers day after day so that these dangers become commonplace. The dangers of Saya's world were as much to be accepted as were the slim comforts. Consequently his harrowing experiences in the hands of the slavers were soon forgotten. Life was good to Saya these days for the one thing he wanted in life had been given to him. By the grace of Allah, as he would say, the great wild horse Khala Hawa was his to own, to ride, to cherish.

However, to Saya's mother Khala Hawa became something of a problem. Often at mealtime she would turn to Saya's father Akim Abou.

"What is with thy son that now even his food is forgotten? Is this horse of his a demon who has cast a spell upon the boy so that he forgets the whereabouts of our tent?"

"Let the boy alone wife," he would say. "He is making of the wild horse one which will someday bring fame to our camp." He would chuckle in his beard and wave an encouraging hand to his wife, then slapping his thigh he would exclaim:

"Ahee! Here is a stallion to father many sons and daughters. In our herd are many fine mares and stallions, but the wild one is such a horse as has never before been seen on the desert. I tell you wife, his sons and daughters will bring much gold in the markets."

But Corza, Saya's lovely mother would go back to her duties shaking her head in pretended sorrow.

"Ah, ah! The men of the Bedouin think only of horses and again horses. What is a poor woman to do but cook the food and watch it grow cold."

But in her heart she was secretly very proud of her stalwart son. Around the tiny camp fires built of camel dung, his feat in capturing the wild stallion and taming it to do his bidding was often repeated and much admiration was accorded the brave boy.

Meanwhile Saya was busy and Nedda was even

busier helping him. Though it must be said that her training equipped her far better to help her mother in the goat-hair tent than to help her brother in the horse herd, she dutifully ran and fetched as Saya called upon her. Now it was a skin-pail of water he needed from the spring, or back to the tent for a clean rag torn from an old and discarded burnoose, next a mane and tail comb carved from a slat of wood, or a stiff camel-hair brush for Khala Hawa's beautiful coat. Nedda loved it for she adored this big brother, and it must be said that Saya was not too much the tyrant. Together they washed out the coat of the magnificent horse, then Saya brushed until it shone like burnished silver. The long flowing white mane and the tail which nearly reached the ground were combed until both hung in soft silky billows. Then the boy and his little sister stood back to examine their handiwork.

"Ahee!" exclaimed the boy. "Was there ever a more beautiful horse, sister?"

Nedda smiled her approval uncertainly for while she knew the importance of a fine horse she had neither the great love nor understanding of horses which would one day make her brother the most famed of all the horsemen in Arabia.

"He is very beautiful brother. You have done well."

But Saya's smile turned to a frown, and with an important little swagger he turned to her.

"Done well? Pah. I have done nothing. The hardest work is yet to be done."

Nedda sighed softly thinking that again she must begin the endless running of errands, and of her tiny legs which were aching with fatigue. But Saya did not call upon her to fetch a thing. Instead he reached under his burnoose and from his girdle he drew a knife. Though it was already keen of edge he selected a stone from the ground and began to whet the edge of the knife against it. Nedda watched with interest and in silence, then ventured:

"Why do you sharpen your knife? It is perhaps to cut some dates? That is good, for I am . . ."

But Saya interrupted with a wave of the knife toward Khala Hawa.

"Look at his feet," he said.

Nedda looked at the shining feet of the beautiful stallion but refrained from further comment. To her they looked exactly the same as the hoofs of the other horses. Khala Hawa however, watched the boy with interest. Half asleep from the pleasant rubbing and brushing the horse was brought to full attention by the sharp zing-zing of the blade against the stone. His tiny ears came erect and pointed toward the sound. His nostrils flared in an attempt to catch any strange scent which might accompany this odd noise. But nothing happened and finally the beautiful head of the horse dropped and his velvety lips sought out and found a few wisps of succulent grass.

Saya tested the knife blade and found it to his satisfaction. Rising from the ground he handed the halter rope to Nedda and admonished her:

"Hold Khala Hawa, Nedda, but not too tightly. Let him have his head free."

Nedda took the rope obediently but asked:

"What will you do Saya?"

Saya pointed to the hoofs of the grey stallion.

"See how long are the hoofs of Khala Hawa? And how frayed are the edges? When he ran wild in the desert he kept them worn well down and smooth at the edges. But now he spends much time in our camp without the need to go far in search of food and the horn of the hoof grows long and I must trim it."

The horse turned his head slowly to watch Saya as he stepped to his side and reached down to lift a foreleg. Obediently the great horse raised his foot at the touch of the boy's hand, but at the first strange pull of the knife blade, Khala Hawa snatched his foot away. Of course it did not hurt, because a horse's hoof can be trimmed as can the fingernails on the human hand. It was not pain which frightened Khala Hawa, but rather the fear of the unknown which never leaves even the best tamed and trained of horses. Saya spoke soothingly to him:

"So my great horse, Saya will not hurt you. So . . . so."

Khala Hawa again presented his foot when Saya reached for it, though this time with some hesitation. Again the knife cut into the horn and this time the horse snorted his fear and snatched his foot away so violently and suddenly that Saya was nearly tumbled to the ground. Patiently Saya persisted but fright grew in Khala Hawa. Finally when he reared back so violently that the halter rope was jerked from Nedda's hand, Saya stopped his efforts, looked sorrowfully once at his fine animal and turned to Nedda.

"So now another lesson my great one must have. Give me the halter rope, Nedda."

Saya led the horse to the shade of a palm tree and tied the rope securely to the trunk. Then from his girdle he drew a short quirt of camel-hide. At once Nedda's eyes opened wide, for she recognized the short camel-hide whip at once.

"You will whip Khala Hawa Saya? But only cruel men whip their horses. Why are you angry with him?"

Saya smiled at her. "I am neither angry nor cruel."

Now the boy stepped to the head of his horse. Slipping the quirt over his wrist he let it dangle there while he stroked the beautiful head gently, and as he caressed the horse he spoke, as much to Khala Hawa as to Nedda.

"It is the way of the world that we learn by pain and pleasure. When we are young our mother and father teach us the way to live. If we do wrong we are punished. If we do well we are rewarded. And so we learn."

Nedda nodded slowly in agreement with this wisdom of her brother. Saya went on.

"Even more is this true of the horse. We can say to ourselves I did wrong and I was punished. The horse cannot do this for you see, he is not even so intelligent as a dog."

Saya emphasized his remarks with a wave of his hand toward the camp where even now the dogs were helping to drive home the flocks of sheep and goats for the night.

"It is for the man to think for his horse. To do the things which are good for the horse." He scowled mildly at Khala Hawa. "And that is why I must now teach this one what is good for him."

Nedda looked a little frightened at the determined expression on her brother's face.

"Will you hurt him greatly, Saya," she asked.

Saya shook his head. "No sister. But as my father has often said, be strong with your horses, though kindly. Remember that a little pain today may save him a great hurt tomorrow."

He spoke to the horse as he stroked the silken nose as though Khala Hawa could understand his words.

"Great one I must trim your hoofs. Look you how badly you stand. If you ran over the sand today you would twist the tendons of your legs . . . perhaps even into the great hurt of which my father spoke. Now . . . stand!"

Again Saya lifted the slender foreleg and again the fine horse permitted it, but at the first touch of the knife the foot disappeared from Saya's grasp. Now however, Khala Hawa's lesson began in earnest. The quirt flashed through the air and landed smartly on his shoulder. The horse snorted in surprise as the lash stung and backed away. Then the boy soothed:

"Stand Khala Hawa! Stand!"

For the next half hour the will and wisdom of the boy were pitted against the strength and fear of the horse. It was Khala Hawa who weakened. Slowly at first and then more rapidly the fine animal began to associate the sting of the quirt with his own obstinacy. When he drew his foot from the boy's grasp the sting of the quirt came to his body, and Saya's voice low but firm and demanding spoke the single word: "Stand! Stand!"

Then the sharp knife cut away with the first sliver of horn. Khala Hawa felt no pain. Trembling with fear but remembering the sting of the quirt he permitted another sliver of hoof to be trimmed away. Now faster and faster could Saya work. Each hoof was more easily worked upon than the last. Khala

Hawa's fear lessened, the trembling stopped finally, and then the task was done. Saya straightened wearily, hands on his aching back to gaze fondly but tiredly at the great horse.

"So you great idiot," he said. "Do not the feet feel better? Look now how squarely you stand to the ground. True my fine one, the shoulder is a little sore, eh? But . . ." Saya shrugged. "I too have been sore in a certain place after a lesson from my father. Tomorrow it will not hurt."

Now from a sack, Saya took barley and spread it before Khala Hawa. The grey horse needed no urging for here was a treat, a new treat in fact, another of the wonderful things which had happened to him through the boy Saya. Delicious food which could never be found the length and breadth of the desert, kind gentle hands to smooth his coat and comb his mane. Khala Hawa was content. Gone was the fear of the knife, already disregarded were the few stings to his shoulder. Khala Hawa's lesson was learned.

Chapter 6

SAYA AND NEDDA trudged wearily across the deserted end of the oasis. Saya had finally begun to think of the dinner growing cold upon the goatskin rug in the tent, and Nedda carefully pointed out to him that all members of the camp except the guards were at the evening meal. Once they reached the tent they cleansed themselves well and entered. Sheik Akim Abou was seated on the goat-skin rug leaning comfortably against the camel saddle as usual. Their mother who heard them coming brought the food which she had been keeping warm over the tiny fire and placed it before them. Her eyes were tender as she looked at her sturdy son and her beautiful little daughter, but her voice was firm as she spoke:

"Now must we talk my son. Now hear me say that with all good will to thy fine horse, he must not take away the honor of thy father's tent. There is a time for each thing to be done, and not again must thou keep thyself and thy sister away at the time for the evening food."

"I am sorry my mother," Saya said. Then he added eagerly: "But so much was to be done for Khala Hawa, and now you should look at him!"

But Akim Abou interrupted: "Though your horse gleam from your grooming with the holy light of the first horse created by Allah, you have still come late to the evening meal, my son. You must learn to apportion to each task a certain time. Too much is a waste, too little a danger."

Smiling at Saya, Akim Abou went on:

"Think of this my son. You are late to the evening meal, therefore you should have started the care of your horse earlier. Should you perhaps undertake a journey in such a fashion to meet a caravan with which you would cross the desert, you would arrive at the appointed place to find the caravan gone on without you. Thus you would be left alone, perhaps even to die."

Saya nodded. His father's voice was kindly, but the

boy knew he was not wasting words. Time to the Arab is nothing, and yet it is everything. He does not count time as we do, in seconds and minutes and hours, with each day seeing some new accomplishment. He will think perhaps in this fashion: "I must travel from this place to that place. How many days I must travel is unimportant. Rather, how much water must I carry to see myself and my animals safely across the desert." The Arab thinks not of time, but simply of survival in his barren world. And food is important.

Nedda was safely tucked in bed and sound asleep. Corza, their mother, busied herself with woman's work, and Saya and his father sat together on the goat-skin rug to talk. Saya's mind was dwelling still on horses, and particularly his own great stallion, and so he related all that he had done that day. His father listened, puffed at the long flexible stem of his water-pipe, and only interrupted occasionally with questions such as:

"In trimming the hoofs of your horse, my son, you did not let the knife touch the frog of the foot?"

"Oh no father. The inner foot of Khala Hawa is perfectly formed and high. To cut the frog would be very harmful."

At this the man would only nod and wait for the boy to go on. Finally Saya paused and gazed for a moment into the little bed of coals which glowed on the tent floor before them. Then he looked at his father.

"We have many animals my father. From the sheep in our flocks comes meat to eat, and wool to clothe ourselves, from the goats also come sustenance and comforts. Our camels give us delicious milk to drink, strong hair and hides from which we make many things. And they carry us great distances in safety. Yet it is the horse we love most. Why is that?"

Akim Abou looked at his thoughtful son, then back to the fire. His voice was low as he spoke.

"Allah il Allah. There is no God but Allah."

Saya looked up in some surprise at the familiar expression. Often had he heard it shouted from the lips of his father's warriors, as mounted on their beautiful, swift war-mares they galloped into battle to fight off an invading enemy. But he waited for his father to continue.

"Is it then my son," Akim Abou asked. "That you think our horses bring us only pleasure? That they do not contribute to our lives? True, when we move our camp, our possessions and ourselves are borne upon the backs of camels while our horses move with us unburdened. But think you, when danger threatens, what animal carries us into battle, and by speed and courage carries us through the fighting and safely home? It is the horse. When the herds are thin and food is desperately needed how do we hunt the swift gazelle? On camel back? Ah no, the horse is the only one to match the speed of our prey. And again, when fatigue overtakes the camel he will work no longer, yet the horse will go on and on until it drops lifeless on the desert floor."

Saya frowned. His father's words were true, he knew, but still the bond between man and horse had not been explained to his fullest satisfaction.

"All this I understand father, yet there must be more. Why did you use the word of God?"

"Because of the legend my son," the man answered. Akim Abou puffed reflectively on his pipe for a moment so that the cooling water in the vase bubbled softly. Then he continued:

"It is said that when Allah created the world, he created all of the animals also, and he made them of the lesser materials. But when he created the horse he called upon the South Wind and spoke to it: 'I will that a creature should proceed from thee. Condense thyself.' And the wind condensed itself and from this substance Allah fashioned the horse. He said further to the horse: 'I have attached good fortune to the forelock of hair that falls between thy eyes. Thou shalt be the Lord of all animals. Men shall follow thee wheresoever thou goest. Good for pursuit as well as flight, thou shall fly without wings.'"

Akim Abou paused for a moment and looked at his son, then he finished:

"Because of the horses' swiftness which sends the air singing past your ears, we call them the 'drinkers of the Winds and Air.' It may be that to preserve this, his noblest of animals, Allah implanted in our hearts a great love so that we would care and administer to the horse as you cared for Khala Hawa this day."

Akim Abou stopped speaking and puffed slowly at his pipe. Saya remained silent. His heart was too full for speech. In his mind he thanked Allah, his God, for this great gift. He thought of Khala Hawa standing with the other beautiful horses under the date palms, his silver coat gleaming in the moonlight. Then he arose, and bidding his father a quiet goodnight he went to his bed. His father sat silently thinking. Through his mind passed many pictures, pictures of horses which had born him safely and swiftly. His eyes saddened as he thought of those which had died in his service, some panting their lifeblood out onto the sand where they had fallen in battle. And he thought of Saya and Khala Hawa. In his mind he saw his son racing across the desert on the back of the magnificent horse. A little smile crossed his lips as the thought passed through his mind that he would like to ride this wonderful mount, but he shook his head slowly as he reminded himself that Khala Hawa had dedicated his life to his son and to no other man. The water pipe bubbled softly and Akim Abou was content for he knew that the great horse would carry his beloved son safely through many dangers with courage and swiftness.

Chapter 7

MANY TIMES the camp of the Bedouin was moved in the next few months. Their flocks of sheep and goats, and the herds of camels and horses cropped down the grass of even a large oasis quickly. Away from the desert they moved, and into the foothills where, though sparse, vegetation did exist. And the hardy Arabian horses, the beautiful fawn colored camels and the wooly sheep grew fat and sleek.

To Saya it was the happiest of times. The great horse Khala Hawa and the boy grew closer and closer until the beautiful grey stallion would hardly permit him out of sight. Perhaps Saya spoiled the horse a bit for his fingers were always seeking out a tender spot behind the ear or reaching up under the long mane to scratch the crown of Khala Hawa's powerful neck. There was always a tid-bit concealed beneath Saya's burnoose; perhaps a handful of barley or a few dried dates which the horse had learned to love.

Nevertheless though he lavished love and affection on the animal, Saya was still a horseman and always was he firm with the great stallion. When night fell and the Bedouin retired to his tent, Khala Hawa was banished to the herd of horses there to spend the night resting and grazing so that he would be fed and ready for the next day's work. But it pleased Saya that when the first rays of the rising sun slanted across the desert seeming to set the sands on fire, Khala Hawa left the herd and came straight to the tent of Akim Abou. There he would stand nickering and thumping his soft muzzle against the side of the tent until Saya awakened and came out to him. Saya would swagger a little as he walked about the camp, the beautiful horse tagging at his heels, for though the Arabian horse is noted for its devotion to its master, no other horse in the camp was so devoted as Khala Hawa.

Many a doughty warrior of the Bedouin chuckled to watch Saya riding Khala Hawa and driving home the sheep for the night. To the great stallion this task had become a game which he seemed to feel had been invented for his own special benefit and pleasure. Almost as quickly as an intelligent dog, Khala Hawa learned to drive the sheep before him. And this he did with all his heart, prancing and dancing, spinning quickly to this side or that to return a wanderer to the flock. Now he would drop his head and with his nose nudge a too-slow ewe or lamb to a faster pace, uttering meanwhile little squeals of pure joy.

It is true that sometimes at night when Saya was asleep Khala Hawa would stand at the edge of the camp and look out over the vast reaches of the moonlit desert. What was in his mind as he sent the ringing cry of the wild stallion echoing across the sand we will never know. If his mind pictured the wild free days when he ruled his kingdom of sand it also must have pictured the comforts and wonders of life in the Bedouin camp with Saya, for never again did the wild horse show any real desire to return to his old life. The story of the wild stallion and his young master travelled far and wide until finally every visitor to the camp asked to see the pair, so they also could marvel at the great stallion's constant and untiring devotion to the boy. Saya was level-headed, but still a boy nevertheless. It must be related here that all this attention turned his head a bit, and he became somewhat conceited and much too proud of his power over the great horse.

Saya was awakened one morning not by his beautiful horse but by his mother.

"Such a lazy one," she said. "Do you intend to sleep all day boy? Come, the flocks await thee. They would be taken to the grazing ground."

Saya rose from his robes, stretched and then looked around puzzled. Something was wrong. Then suddenly he realized what it was. There was no familiar nicker to call him outside the tent. Quickly he stepped into the open and looked about. But his stallion was nowhere to be seen.

A cold fear descended on Saya and without waiting for his morning meal he ran to the edge of the camp where the horses were pastured. In Saya's mind there was only one thought; that the wild call had taken his beloved horse back into the sea of sand which had once been his home. Gone now was all swagger and conceit, and in Saya's heart was a prayer to Allah that if the wild had called to Khala Hawa, the power of their love for each other would bring the great horse back to him. And then he came to the pasture and saw Khala Hawa. He was standing to one side of the main herd, for the proud grey stallion had long since established himself as its ruler, and with him stood a beautiful filly, a young mare which belonged to Akim Abou, Saya's father. Saya recognized the filly at once for he had helped break her to ride and to train her to the reins. Her name was Ja Mi Li, which in Arabic means "the clever and beautiful one." And well did she deserve her name. The color of the Arabian horse is always grey, chestnut or bay, but Ja Mi Li was the color of very dark, rich cream, almost a light fawn color, and her long flowing mane and tail were of the purest white as were Khala Hawa's. Perhaps this color was a throwback to an unknown barb in the ancestry of the horse, but in all other respects, she was a nearly perfect specimen of the classic Arabian Horse, of which Khala Hawa was so typical. At any rate, the sight sent a shade of anger

over Saya's face, for he had grown used to the constant attention of the grey stallion.

"Khala Hawa! Come to me!" Saya's voice was insistent.

Khala Hawa looked toward the boy, stretched his head high in the air and nickered loudly. But he did not leave the side of the beautiful young mare. Saya walked up to the horse, placed a restraining hand on his neck, and taking the forelock in his other hand attempted to lead Khala Hawa to the camp. But, planting his forefeet firmly the stallion gently shook himself loose and returned to the side of Ja Mi Li. Now he looked back to Saya and with gentle nickers pleaded with the boy to come to him.

But Saya was piqued. Such treatment from his devoted horse was unthinkable. He turned sharply on his heel and hurried back to camp, unmindful of the pleading calls which Khala Hawa sent after him. Back in his father's tent he sat down sulkily to his morning meal, his face as dark as one of the thunderclouds which, in the rainy season hung over their camp in the foothills. Akim Abou was already about his duties. Nedda had gone with the women of the camp to the spring for the day's water supply, and only Corza, Saya's mother was left in the tent.

"Eat of the food, my son," she said. Then being a wise woman she waited until Saya's temper would permit him to speak. Finally he did, explosively.

"Such a thing! First he does not come to my tent. Now he does not even come to me."

Innocently Corza asked: "Who does not come, and why?"

Saya was a little indignant that she should ask such a question.

"Khala Hawa, of course, my mother. He was not at the tent to waken me this morning."

Corza shrugged. "Perhaps," she suggested, "he was otherwise busy."

Saya stormed: "He has no right to do as he did. First he does not come to the tent. I go to him, but he will not follow me. True he called to me, but still he walked away. I will not have it!"

His mother hid a smile behind her hand. Then assuming a disinterested voice: "Thou must have suffered great humiliation, my son, when thy horse left thee to return to the mare's side."

Saya looked up quickly, startled.

"How did you know he went to a mare?"

"Did he not?" his mother asked.

Saya nodded. "The filly of father's. Ja Mi Li."

Now Corza dropped her pretense and came to her son to seat herself beside him on the goat-skin rug. She knew now that the time had come for her to speak.

"Be not angry with thy great horse, Saya, for he only follows the will of Allah. Did you not say that Khala Hawa called you to come to him? To join him at the side of the mare, Ja Mi Li? Know this my son. It is not that he has turned against you. It is only that another dear one has come into his life."

Saya turned to her, puzzled but interested.

"I do not understand, my mother. I thought he turned against me."

Corza patted his hand and smiled gently.

"Listen then, my son, and perhaps you will understand." She looked away as though to search for the words she needed. Then, speaking slowly and tenderly she continued.

"It is the will of Allah that all the creatures of this earth find companionship, one with the other. Many years ago when your father was a young man he rode across the sands to the tent of my father. There he asked me to go with him. This I did gladly and because I did a child was born . . . you, our son. This is the way of all the creatures, of men, of the jackal, of the lion, of the horse. To each creature Allah gives a mate, and from these matings come the children of the earth. Do not be troubled that now the affections of your horse are divided between you and the beautiful Ja Mi Li. For one day Allah will give to them a little one to bring them happiness just as you, my son, have brought happiness to your father and me."

Now Corza rose wisely and left the tent. Saya did not move and the food before him was untouched. But now his eyes were shining with joy! The son of Khala

Hawa! Or perhaps even better, the daughter! For was he not growing up, and the daughter of Khala Hawa would grow up, and he would need a war-mare when he joined the ranks of the warriors. Did not every Bedouin need a war-mare? Was it not better on the night raids when so much depended on stealth to ride a mare rather than a stallion which might send its ringing challenge to the horses of the enemy camp, and thus give away the position of the Bedouin? But on second thought, a son would be best. Next a daughter.

Slowly Saya rose from the tent-floor and walked again toward the pasture. No anger was in him now, only a great joy. Gone was the conceit and in its place was the humbleness of wisdom, and a new awareness of the wonders of creation. This time it was the boy who learned the lesson, and his great grey stallion was the teacher.

Chapter 8

WE MUST GO BACK in our story to the day when the hulking Kalim helped his fallen chief, Hassan, to the spring in the oasis, and bathed the terrible wound inflicted by Khala Hawa. It was only a stroke of fortune that Hassan was yet alive, for as the flashing hoofs of the big stallion flew to crush his skull, Hassan turned just enough to receive a glancing blow across the forehead, rather than the full force of the mighty horse's strength. But it was enough. Hassan looked around, then, at the shambles of what had once been the camp of a strong raiders' band, and saw only dead men. His valuable slaves, taken in many hard raids, his personal possessions, his food stores . . . gone, all gone! And all because of a Bedouin boy and a devil horse. Then and there he swore vengeance on Saya and Khala Hawa.

In the next few weeks, Saya did not know how often his life had hung by the proverbial thread. How could he know as he rode his great stallion across the desert sand that Hassan and Kalim lay in wait behind a sand dune. But if fortune and fate had served Hassan well, they also saved the boy and his great horse from the bullets of the two would-be assassins. One time the distance was too far for them to shoot. The next time Saya was followed by herdsmen from his own camp. Still another time Hassan held his trigger finger because Saya rode at a gallop, and the blinding speed of Khala Hawa made a death-shot impossible, and a wounded boy would send the Bedouin scouring the desert for the ambushers. Rage mounted in Hassan's heart, but finally Kalim, though he was not too bright, made the angry man see the facts.

"Hassan," he said. "I am only a simple man of great strength, but of no quickness of mind. I will follow a strong leader into the jaws of death. Thus I have followed you. But no longer can I follow you."

Hassan dismissed Kalim's plaint with a wave of the hand. He had no respect at all for the big man's thoughts.

"Pah," he said. "Without me to think for you you would starve to death."

Kalim answered: "Always has this been true, and that is why I have followed you. Now it is your thinking which will see us starve to death. We have left only enough food for three days."

Thus it was that Hassan was brought to his senses, and though a cruel one, he was also a shrewd man. They left the desert then, and that part of the Nejd as the Arabian desert is named, saw no more of them for a long time.

Now Hassan began to visit his old haunts. Followed always by the huge Kalim he turned up in drinking places and coffee houses in many towns and each time he left word with those who knew him that he was seeking men to form a new band of raiders. But then it came to him as a surprise that men who knew him, and men who had only heard of him, refused to join his banner. Yes, word of Hassan's defeat at the hands of chained slaves, and a single stallion had spread before him, the length and breadth of Arabia. It was believed by the superstitious men of this underworld that a demon had fastened to Hassan who would bring only ill luck to him, and to all who followed him. Weeks went past, and the only band which Hassan had was the hulking Kalim.

Now gloom came over the bearded slaver, and he took to sitting longer and longer in the drinking places consuming much wine. Night after night, befuddled by too much wine, he would stagger from the cafes into the streets. Sometimes he would reach the miserable room to which his poverty held him, and often he would fall in the streets to lie sleeping until the wine fumes cleared from his brain. No longer did Hassan think clearly. Only did he brood over his fancied wrongs. His hate for Saya and Khala Hawa grew and grew, but now so great was his urge for revenge, and so small his chance of accomplishing it, that his hatred encompassed the entire tribe of Bedouins. In his dreams of revenge he would say:

"I will take vengeance on the Bedouin. Hundreds will fall to my guns and my swords. I shall level their tents and place their women and children in my slave line. And the first in that line shall be the boy Saya!"

Thus he would talk to himself until his hatred of the Bedouin became a thing of fire consuming his reason. But luck as it often does, favored Hassan the cruel one.

One night having drunk too much wine as usual, he fell asleep by the roadside and there he was found as the small caravan of a wealthy merchant chanced to pass. It was the merchant Mussadin returning from the markets where he had sold his tapestries and cloths. He was returning to his home with his saddlebags heavy with gold. The bazaars had been good to Mussadin that day and being a kindly man anyway, he was doubly filled with a spirit of good will. He commanded his two servants to pick Hassan up from the gutter and place him on the lightly loaded camel. The passive Hassan was taken to the merchant's house and there put to bed. It was Mussadin's plan to speak with Hassan in the morning to see if he could not help the bearded slaver to find himself and return to the ways of decency, for the merchant, despite his great wealth, was a devout Mohammedan who truly lived within the precepts of goodness.

It is a shame that Mussadin did not realize he was aiding one of the most vicious men in the land, and not as he supposed a poor overburdened man who had turned to wine to forget his sorrows. Hassan wakened, shook his head to clear it and took stock of his surroundings. It was late at night and the house was quiet, the servants and the family of the merchant having gone to bed. The slaver slipped out of the bed and moved cautiously through the house, for Hassan had lost none of the stealth acquired in hundreds of raids. Seeing a light in a room ahead of him, Hassan investigated and saw seated at a table his host, Mussadin, and before the merchant on the table were many stacks of gold pieces. The man was working on his accounts. Hassan almost cried out in surprise, but contained himself, and prepared to make the most of his situation.

Hassan at no time was to be called a merciful man, and now his mind brutalized by his own vengeful thoughts he did not even pause to consider that the man who sat with his back turned was his benefactor. From his girdle Hassan drew a long, thin knife. Moving with the softness and grace of a cat the unkempt slaver easily approached the chair where Mussadin sat absorbed in his accounts. In a second it was all over. Quickly Hassan scooped the gold into sacks. In a trice, he was gone.

It was a new Hassan who now appeared in the coffee shops. His garments were of the finest silk. At his girdle hung a bejewelled purse, beautifully embossed and made of shagreen, and it jingled with the gold coins it contained. The long thin knife now gone, was replaced by a dagger which held a sparkling ruby of great size in the hilt. Thus, word spread quickly that the fortunes of Hassan had changed. And indeed they had. No longer did the slaver drink too freely of the wine, for in his own mind he was suddenly restored to his former eminence. He did not however recruit a large band all at once. Many men did continue to hesitate, but some joined with him. The worthy Kalim was the first to return, and with him came a dozen men as brutish as himself.

Now Hassan procured mounts for himself and his men, and they rode out onto the desert to begin this new career. If it was not a large band, it was a capable one, for each member was a murderer many times over, and none of them would have hesitated at any crime. Slaving was Hassan's favorite line, for the profits were large, but with so small a band slaving

was out of the question. His band, though desperate, was too small to even consider a raid on a village where perhaps two hundred hard-fighting warriors must be conquered. To steal the women and children of a village required many men. Hassan therefore turned to raiding caravans. Many an unwary merchant who ventured to cross the desert without waiting for the large heavily guarded commercial caravans, was never heard from again. The fame of Hassan, and the wealth of his band, grew. One by one cutthroats from town and desert came to his camp to ask admission into his band. If they could prove their mettle they were accepted and thus the band grew large. It was inevitable that one day Kalim, who by now was first lieutenant to Hassim, should come to his chief with a new worry.

"The men grumble, Hassan," reported Kalim. "There are now too many of us in the band."

"The loot from our last caravan raid was not enough to satisfy everyone, is that it?" Hassan asked.

"That is it." Kalim looked shamefaced. "Even I found it not enough, and I am easily satisfied as you Hassan, and . . ."

But Hassan interrupted with a wave of his hand. "You will never be satisfied," he said. "That great belly of yours calls for fine foods and sweetmeats too often."

But Kalim was not to be put off.

"The news is bad Hassan. The men speak of leaving you if you do not plan better so that more loot comes to them."

Hassan chuckled in his beard.

"The news is not bad, Kalim. Indeed it is very very good. Are you not tired of raiding the miserable caravans which cross the desert? Are you not tired of unloading stolen camels to find dried dates where you hoped to find silks and satins? Yes, Kalim. We will give up raiding caravans. I am myself tired of it."

Kalim was baffled. What was this Hassan proposed? That raiding was unprofitable, and that they give it up? Did Hassan, then, expect Kalim to go to work?

"Why do you think I sought to build up my band, Kalim? Today we have nearly a hundred men. Send them out to spread the news that Hassan is about to bring great wealth to any man who will join him. We need another hundred men. Go. Go quickly and find the men. When they join us I will tell them where next we meet."

Kalim was excited at these stirring words, but he had another thought.

"Another hundred men, Hassan. But what is your plan?"

Hassan's lip curled and he looked far away as he answered.

"Hassan returns to his first love . . . the taking of slaves! Go! Go quickly! Find the men I need. Now they will be glad to join the band of Hassan."

Hassan was right. Again the word spread rapidly and this time men flocked to join with him. Hassan's reputation had grown in stature, and he was now a man of considerable fame among those of the underworld, and ill-fame with the travellers of the desert. They were particular, this time, were Hassan and Kalim, and only those proven to be brave and ruthless were admitted. As each new applicant was accepted, he was surprised to be given directions which sent him far across the Nejd to a tiny oasis only a hundred miles or so from the foothills. Indeed, so tiny was it that it could hardly be called an oasis, and few of the men had ever heard of it. It was hardly more than a moist spot in the desert, where barely enough water seeped up through a small formation of rocks to furnish sustenance to a few scraggly palms. However, here Hassan set up his camp, moving the main body of his band to await the coming of the new men. Hassan delighted to sit at ease in the entrance of his tent, watching them coming in twos and threes, their weary mounts hurrying to the rest they knew awaited them.

Kalim joined him there with questions.

"Hassan, why do we skulk in this spot? If we are to take slaves why are we not journeying to Africa where villages await our raiding? There are no slaves here in the middle of the desert."

Hassan's lip curled in contempt.

"Kalim you were ever a fool. When will you learn to use only that blundering body of yours? I will provide the brain and do the thinking for this band."

"That I always do, Hassan," he shrugged. "But sometimes your thoughts are very hard to follow. I

only know that we will not find slaves in the middle of the desert."

Hassan's evil grin widened and he answered:

"You have much to learn Kalim. One hundred miles from here to the north, three hundred prime slaves, young strong women and children, beautiful of face, await our taking. They will bring fancy prices when we take them to be sold into harems and kitchens."

Kalim's eyes bulged at this news. Hassan went on.

"The camp of Abou is there in the foothills. And is there a more beautiful woman than those of the Bedouin? Or a sturdier slave?"

The terrible scar on the forehead of Hassan flamed and pulsed as he spoke, for again he thought of the flint-hard hoofs of the great grey stallion, and he saw them flash through the air to strike him down. But Kalim shared none of his chief's enthusiasm.

"The camp of Akim Abou," he gasped. "Are you mad, Hassan? He has as many men as we have and the Bedouin fight! Each man is a thousand devils!"

Hassan's eyes rolled heaven-ward as though to question the wisdom of Allah for sending such a dolt to walk this earth. Then directing a stern look toward Kalim he spoke as though explaining a simple lesson to a child.

"Kalim, I see you will never learn. Therefore do not tire my ear with your dull questions. Think you I would risk my newly formed band in a fight with the

Bedouin warriors? I have a plan, fool. And when that plan is put into being we shall simply walk into the camp of the Bedouins and put the chains on those we wish to take."

It was all too much for Kalim's dull mind to comprehend, so he simply nodded in agreement. Hassan waved toward the camp.

"Who have we who are skilled in the art of deceit?" he asked. Then without waiting for Kalim's answer, he went on. "Send to me the two men Nari and Rasha. These are most accomplished liars. Sometimes even do they deceive me."

Kalim nodded again, made as though to speak, but stopped and shook his head in puzzlement. Then he went to the camp to fetch the two men for Hassan.

Hassan was ready to execute his plan.

Chapter 9

SAYA WALKED SLOWLY across the rocky ground where as far as his eye could see, the area was dotted with grazing animals. Here a horse, there a camel, here a sheep with a lamb by its side. It was not that the herds were vast, it was rather due to sparse vegetation that the animals wandered far apart to graze. Then suddenly Saya stopped walking, and a smile came to his lips. Two animals grazed close together and the two were his beloved Khala Hawa and the beautiful mare Ja Mi Li. The boy's sharp whistle brought both of them galloping to a sliding halt before him which sent a cloud of dust skyward. The grey stallion was sleek and fine. His great muscles rippled as he pranced about Saya pretending to nip, and probing with his silky muzzle for the treat of barley which he knew would be forthcoming. However, Ja Mi Li stood quietly, her eyes misty bright, her tiny ears pointed sharply forward. These days Ja Mi Li was not inclined to frisk. She was heavy with the foal soon to be born and she carried herself with dignity and care. Saya looked at them both with pride then he playfully slapped Khala Hawa but so suddenly that the horse, which had been nuzzling him, shied violently, snorting with surprise. Saya's laugh rang out and the grey stallion came quickly back to him, reassured.

"Lazy ones," said the boy. "You stand about and eat and eat. Today you will work.

Turning to the stallion, Saya pointed to Ja Mi Li.

"Look you," he said. "Here is one who must exercise. Strength must be in her limbs so that she may impart strength to your son."

Now he shook an admonitory finger at the stallion who eyed him closely.

"Not hard work you understand. We will be careful that no injury comes to her. But we will move across the desert easily for a time and thus she will keep her strength."

Khala Hawa did not respond. He was very busy. As the boy continued to talk, the grey horse lost interest, and began again to nuzzle at the corded girdle which encircled the boy's waist, and his sharp white teeth worried at the knot. Suddenly to Saya's surprise the knot loosened and the girdle fell to the ground spilling the small sack of barley which had been secured there. With a little squeal of joy Khala Hawa pounced upon the spilled grain, and then curling his upper lip he whinnied loudly as though laughing at the trick he had played on his master. Saya recovered from his surprise, laughed, and rubbed the sleek nose of the stallion.

"So ho," he said. "This is what I earn for teaching tricks to you, eh? Now that you can untie knots you will steal the grain from my girdle. You will pay for that my beautiful one."

Saya slipped the handsomely braided bridle over the horse's head, carefully arranging the colorful tassels to hang free. Tossing the reins over Khala Hawa's withers he turned to Ja Mi Li and slipped a head-stall over her delicate head. To this he fastened a lead-line. About to mount Khala Hawa, Saya turned to see his little sister Nedda running as though her chubby little legs were steel springs. Out of breath and pink of cheek she dashed up to him.

"Oh Saya," she panted. "Mother said you had gone to ride and I hurried so I would not miss you."

Saya frowned, for though he loved his little sister and enjoyed her company, today he had work to do. It was true that Ja Mi Li needed mild exercise even though her foal was soon to be born, and Saya was determined to supervise that exercise so that the mare would keep her strength, but keep it in safety."

"You should not have come today, little sister," Saya said. "I have work to do. Now, hurry back to our mother in the tent."

Turning he began to adjust the halter on Ja Mi Li's head. But Nedda was not to be put off.

"Today," she announced in a determined voice, "I am going with you. You have not taken me in a long time."

Saya turned to her in some annoyance, but before he could speak a new thought struck him. He pursed his lips, furrowed his brow and in other ways tried to look important. Of course this play-acting was intended to impress only this small sister of his, yet, actually the judgment of an expert horseman was being called into play. He looked critically at Ja Mi Li. He picked up each of her feet and examined them closely. He ran his hands over the tendons of her legs, and smoothed the muscles of her well built fore-arms. Then he turned to Nedda and spoke.

"Little one," he said pompously. "Is your courage with you this day?"

Nedda, never sure whether her brother was joking or serious, merely nodded.

"Good," said Saya. He pointed to Ja Mi Li. "Have you then the courage to ride this wild mare?"

Nedda giggled for Ja Mi Li was as gentle as a pet kitten.

"Wild mare!" she answered. "The only wild thing in this mare is the grass she has eaten."

Saya laughed at her joke then he explained.

"Nedda I like not the way Ja Mi Li handles herself. She is light-made, with very fine legs, and she is very heavy. She will bear a colt, rather than a filly, and he will be a big one, that I know. I have watched her move and she has grown lazy with the weight in her body. She does not pick up her feet, but rather drags them. Today I will exercise her, but I think it would be good if she carried a little weight."

Nedda's eyes rounded in surprise.

"You want me to ride her when she is so soon to foal?"

Saya nodded: "You will ride well forward on her withers. Your weight will be as nothing to her, but just enough so perhaps she will pick up her feet and thus benefit from the exercise."

He frowned, thinking the while, then nodded.

"Yes, we must get her action higher. It will be good for her. We will go slowly and she will not be hurt."

Now with Saya's help Nedda quickly scrambled to Ja Mi Li's back, and gathered in the halter rope, though there was no need to guide the gentle mare who would simply follow Khala Hawa. Saya vaulted to the back of Khala Hawa and moving at a fast walk they left the grazing grounds and headed for the open desert. As they moved out of the oasis, Saya turned to look back at the beautiful mare who closely followed the lead of his stallion and watched her action critically. He was pleased at what he saw. The weight of tiny Nedda was negligible to a horse used to carrying ten times as much, but the slight weight, plus the good psychology of carrying a rider were the proper prescription. Ja Mi Li picked up her dainty feet with just the suggestion of a prance and Saya knew that the day's exercise would benefit her greatly.

Later, Saya permitted them a short easy canter which ended atop a sand dune, from which they could see the camp in the oasis far behind them. As they stopped here to rest, Ja Mi Li drew close to Khala Hawa's side, and laid her delicate head across the great stallion's withers, directly in the lap of Saya. It was a favorite habit of the beautiful mare, for as they rested thus, Saya's strong brown fingers scratched the ears, and combed the silken mane, and Ja Mi Li had she been a cat, would have purred with pleasure. It was Nedda who glanced behind them, and gave a little squeal of fright!

"Saya! Behind you! Strangers come!"

Saya turned quickly, ready to put their horses into a run for the camp if necessary. But he was reassured when he saw that the long rifles of the strangers remained peacefully in the scabbards attached to their saddles. He counselled Nedda to wait without fear. The horsemen approached, stopped nearby and faced them. Then one spoke:

"I am Rasha," he said. "This one is Nari. We seek the camp of Akim Abou. Can you direct us?"

Saya nodded. "It is just below us. We return there now. Follow us. Akim Abou is my father, the Sheik."

The return trip to camp was short, for on their ride, Saya had led them in a great circle. The children led the way to their father's tent, and at their call Akim Abou came out to greet the strangers. At once they were taken into the tent for coffee and to be served a small portion of bread and salt, for this is the Bedouin's proffered token of friendship.

The visit of strangers to their camp was enthralling to Nedda and Saya. Leaving Ja Mi Li and Khala Hawa to return to the pasture alone, the boy and girl crept close to the tent to listen. They heard the voice of the stranger who called himself Rasha speak.

"We are come from the camel market," he said. "Men have come from Egypt to purchase camels for the army's use. Many of their beasts were killed in a battle there, and that is why they must purchase more though this is not the time to purchase camels. Because it is not the time of market they are prepared to pay a price much higher than the ordinary market. Have you camels to sell?"

Akim Abou smiled for this was rare news.

"In my camp are many prime camels," he said. "It is seldom we have the chance to sell for a price higher than the market. I think the men of my camp will be glad to sell their animals to these buyers."

That night wine made of the date was drunk to celebrate the arrival of these good tidings and many a sheep was roasted whole and eaten. Yet the next day the camp was aroused early. The two visitors Rasha and Nari mounted their horses and left while the men of the camp hurried their preparations to take their camels to the town for offer to the unexpected buyers.

Akim Abou was a wise man and prudent, and for many years he had guided the people of his camp well. Under his guidance they had prospered, their camp had grown strong and no marauding tribes had dared to attack them. Consequently a long time of safety and peace had dulled their thinking and they were unprepared for a trick. Akim Abou as he led his men out of the camp, driving their camel herd between them, did not for a moment suspect that from a nearby sand dune the two false messengers, Rasha and Nari watched them go. As the long line of Bedouins and their drove of camels moved away from the camp, Nari spoke:

"The trick has worked. There can hardly be one fighting man left in the camp."

And Rasha answered: "We had best hurry back and report to Hassan. I think he will want to attack the camp quickly while it is unprotected, and long before the Bedouin warriors learn there is no camel market. Come."

And thus the plan of Hassan was consummated.

Chapter 10

THE MOON DROPPED lower and lower in the skies until finally its slanting rays on the sand dunes threw long black shadows across the desert floor interspersed only occasionally with patches of bright light. Had there been anyone to watch they might have seen ghostly horsemen slip across these bright patches to melt into the shadows beyond. In such fashion did the minions of Hassan approach the camp of the Bedouin. The hoofs of their horses were swathed in rags to muffle the tread and like so many wraiths the assassins closed in around the sleeping camp and took up positions to await the coming of dawn.

In the desert, night and day exchange rapidly. One moment it was pitch black, then a quick fading into grey, and suddenly the sun shot out from behind a tall dune and the camp of the Bedouins was aflame with light. A single rifle shot rang out and then the foothills were filled with yelling demons. The camp of Akim Abou was caught completely by surprise, for with only the old men and boys to stand guard many had nodded at their posts, and sprang awakened to their feet only at the raiders' signal for the attack. Even so the raiders had no easy time of it.

Saya was wide awake and out of his sleeping robes in an instant. He snatched up the rifle which was always kept loaded and conveniently at hand. Slinging the pouch of ammunition over his shoulder he ran out of the tent. But for all his quickness the raiders, mounted on swift horses, were already inside the camp. Saya flung himself aside just in time to avoid being ridden down by a wild-eyed horse whose rider deliberately reined across Saya's path. This was the way of the raiders. Inspire fear and dread, and the battle is half won! But not Saya nor any of the others were to be frightened so easily. Quickly the women and children gathered in the prearranged places of protection behind the great rocks which were scattered about the sloping hillside. Then the older boys, Saya among them, and the old men who were not too enfeebled with age or illness, took up shelter behind

any shelter from which they might conveniently aim and fire their long rifles. Such maneuvers helped to discount the raiders' advantage in being mounted. Indeed, occasionally the raider astride his horse was at some disadvantage for, mounted, he was quite visible where otherwise the rocky terrain would have offered better concealment from the riflemen.

The Bedouin fought well and bravely. Saya loaded and fired his father's spare rifle until the barrel grew hot in his hands. The boy was a fine shot and many of the raiders were put out of the fight by his well aimed bullets. It is true that most of them fell of lesser wounds only, for to achieve a heart or a head shot when the target is mounted on a galloping horse is purely a matter of good fortune.

But it was all to no avail. The raiders were for the most part younger men and strong, while the defenders were after all feeble old men and young boys. There could only be one ending. Riding hard, the raiders sought out each place of defense and, closing in from all sides, soon conquered the single defender of that place. Saya himself fell from a treacherous blow as a rifle butt struck him from behind. It was characteristic of the raiders that the young strong boys were struck down with rifle butt or club, while the old men were dispatched with bullet or sword. The raiders knew their business well. The old men and women were useless to them. Not only were they worthless on the auction block but their aged feebleness would have only slowed down the progress of the caravan. Hassan himself had given the order to kill the old ones mercilessly but that none of the younger women and children be harmed. That any of the old ones were saved at all was due to the courageous stoicism of the Bedouin. The wounded, though their bodies were wracked with the pain of their hurts, forced themselves to lie on the ground as still as death itself. For the slightest movement on their part would have brought a quick bullet, or a speedy thrust of the sword.

The fight to possess the Bedouin camp was a short one as such fights usually go but it was still too long for Hassan who sat his horse in a protected place from which he could follow the progress of the fighting. Now as the fight slowed down he turned to Kalim and spoke.

"The fight takes far longer than it should Kalim. Are the new men of our band poor fighters then?"

"Indeed no, Hassan," was Kalim's quick answer. "I myself have gone into the fighting again and again. We fight only boys and old men, but even so they fight as would the demons of the Lower Regions! Even the women fight!"

Hassan's thin smile was cruel.

"So it would seem. The fight is gone from them now. We will form the slave lines. Send a man to order the chains prepared."

"At once Hassan."

Kalim turned to one of the waiting couriers and with a few words sent him streaking away. Then he turned back to Hassan and his low ape-like brow was furrowed in thought.

"I wonder at thy haste, Hassan. Thou hast fears?"

"Fear?" Hassan's face contorted with rage. "I fear nothing. But would we not be fools to delay our march until the Bedouins return to give us another fight? They will not be fooled for long, and they will return here with speed."

Kalim looked over his shoulder fearfully. He had no stomach to face the fierce Bedouin warriors who would rage like a hive of angry bees when they found their camp ravaged. Hassan touched heels to his horse's side and moved towards the fight which by now had been reduced to an occasional shot. He wanted to observe for himself the capture of the slaves and the placing of them in the chain line. He wanted to make certain of one slave, and that one was the boy Saya. The long red scar on his forehead grew scarlet with his angry thoughts and again he turned to Kalim who rode beside him.

"The horse," he said. "The grey stallion. You have not forgotten my orders about him?"

"I have not forgotten," Kalim answered. "I have sent men to take him. From what I have heard of this horse it will take many men to conquer him."

"No mind if it takes fifty men," Hassan retorted.

"See that the horse is taken. Go. Attend to it yourself. I will watch over the chaining of the slaves."

Again the desert saw a long line of slaves formed as the women and children of the Bedouin were shackled together. The slavers wasted no time. The bodies of the old men and women which were strewn over the ground from one end of the camp to the other were left to the vultures, which already had begun to circle overhead. Many of these fallen ones were yet alive, but so motionless did they lie in the broiling sun that it was not worth the effort to seek out those still alive and dispatch them. Hassan took a fiendish delight in directing the activities of the raiders delegated to lock the chains on the new slaves. He singled out Saya and his mother and saw to it that these two led the line of captives. Catching up a long lashed whip from the hand of one of his men he held it before Saya and spoke:

"You will lead the line in the march, boy, you and your mother. You will set the pace and it will be a fast pace or you will feel this lash a thousand times."

Then curling the long lash behind him he brought it expertly across Saya's shoulders once and once across the shoulders of Corza. Though neither Saya nor Corza uttered a sound at the cutting blows, Hassan turned away pleased with himself. Kalim rode up now, his burnoose dishevelled, sweat streaking his ugly face.

The grey horse is captured, Hassan," he shouted

with glee. "Ahee! A devil horse it is. Four men with crossed ropes hold it, but finally it is subdued. Ahhh, what beautiful horses the Bedouin own. We will take many of them. . . ."

But Hassan interrupted.

"We will take only the grey stallion. He it is who merits my vengeance. We have many fine slaves. We have no time to waste on horses. Start the march!"

Now the sharp crack of whips echoed among the dunes like rifle shots, echoed in turn by the cries of those whose flesh was laid open by the lash. There could be no protest, and slowly the line began to move

across the sands like a writhing snake. But even this did not satisfy the sadistic impulses of the slavers. Again and again the long-lashed whips cracked out and many a burnoose was to be cut to shreds and the flesh beneath reduced to a quivering mass before the caravan halted for the night.

The wily Hassan knew all the tricks of his rotten business. He moved away from the camp in a different direction from that in which he had come. Behind the line of slaves were posted four horsemen who dragged heavy robes behind their mounts. As these

robes passed over the ground they smoothed out the sand carved by the passage of many feet. Hassan knew that with this help the ever-present desert wind would finish the job, and before the day was half over the tracks of the caravan would be gone and the slaves and their captors swallowed in the desert.

Hour after hour the captive Bedouins trudged through the wasteland, the heavy dragging sand and the broiling sun taking full toll of their strength. Again and again a small child or a woman heavy with child would falter. No helping hand from another slave was permitted them, instead the lash, striking out with unerring accuracy, would flick a bit of flesh from back or thigh. With a little moan of pain the fallen one would rise and stumble forward again.

Hassan was cruel and without mercy, but in his way he was a good business man. He knew well the value of his caravan. He correctly estimated the strength of the marchers, and before the gruelling trek should bring death to even one valuable slave he halted for his first camp. Wisely, as he moved to the attack with his main band, he had sent to this camp a few men, taking the pack animals and the supplies. The site for this first camp was a fairly large oasis well supplied with water and vegetation for many animals. Here Hassan meant to fit out for the many miles of pure desert which lay between him and the slave market.

There was much cracking of whips and rattling of chains as the slave line was halted. The chained captives dropped to the ground like dead men their eyes closed against the torture in their bodies. A few of the stronger ones were freed from the line and leg irons were put upon them. These were put to the task of preparing a meager meal for themselves and their companions in misery. It pleased the brutal Hassan to take Saya and his mother to be his personal servants. Every menial task was allotted them and more than once a short rhinoceros-hide whip which was always in his hand was laid across their shoulders. Finally, tired of his cruel sport the slaver left his tent and Corza dropped sobbing to the ground. Saya put his arms around her.

"My mother," he said. "Do not further weary yourself with grieving. Soon my father and his men will return and come to our help."

Corza shook her head.

"You are a boy of the desert, Saya. You saw the slavers wipe away our trail. Not knowing our direction your father could search the desert for years and not discover our whereabouts."

Saya's mouth tightened for he knew his mother spoke the truth.

"Do not give up hope nevertheless, my mother," he soothed. "We will find a way."

The great grey horse, Khala Hawa suffered also, for

he was no less a prisoner than Saya. He had fought like the furies when first the slavers had tried to capture him until finally so many ropes encircled his neck that they stood out from him like spokes from a wheel. Then, with four strong ropes each in the hands of a powerful man mounted on a sturdy horse, holding him, Khala Hawa was forced to submit. Even then, and for many miles of the cruel march the great horse lashed out against his captors until his body was white with lather. The reputation of Khala Hawa had spread far and wide over the desert, and the men who were his captors took no chances. The big stallion finally had no choice. He had to go where they led him.

By the time they reached the camp the captors of Khala Hawa were convinced that they had finally broken the spirit of the big stallion. Only one rope tied him to a tree, though it was a very stout rope to be sure. The grey horse acted docile enough, for within the limits of his intelligence he had recognized the futility of further fight against such unequal odds. Furthermore, Khala Hawa retained many of his wild instincts, one of which was the ability to rest and restore his body under the most trying circumstances. Consequently he stood quietly enough cropping at the short green grass within the length of his tie-rope. Seeing him so quiet, apparently resigned to captivity his captors went about other duties leaving him to his own devices.

It was when darkness came and Saya did not appear with a tid-bit and gentle fingers to caress him that Khala Hawa became restless. Once or twice he backed off violently but the sturdy rope held. The big horse had learned well about the ropes, and great welts on his massive neck testified to the severity of his lesson. But, now his soft muzzle worried at the length of rope, finally finding the knot which held it securely to the tree. To Khala Hawa a knot was much the same whether it be in a tie-rope or Saya's girdle and at the familiar feel he immediately tested it with his sharp teeth.

Khala Hawa was in many ways remarkably intelligent even as Arabian horses go, but he was still a horse with all the limitations of a horse's mind. His actions were based on past memories, and associations, both pleasant and unpleasant. He worried at the knot because in his simple way he associated it with a pleasant happening in the past. To say that he knowingly tried to untie it would be wrong, but nevertheless he continued to tug and pull at it until suddenly the knot opened and Khala Hawa stood free. Now the great horse turned to look for Saya as he had so often done before, but the unfamiliar surroundings stopped him. He had no scent of Saya to follow, no familiar landmark to seek out. When Saya did not immediately appear he did what any horse would do, he moved to a greener patch of grass, dropped his head and continued his meal. True he looked up impatiently a few times, and whinnied sharply as though to reprove Saya for his tardiness, but as the grass was tender and he was hungry, Khala Hawa continued to graze.

One of the men delegated to guard the great horse had, perhaps, a stronger sense of duty than the other three. At any rate, he chose to go to the place where Khala Hawa had been tethered to check on his charge. The sight of the grey stallion free and grazing far from his picket-tree brought an involuntary shout from the man, and his instant reaction was a quick movement toward the grazing animal. At the sound of the voice Khala Hawa raised his head with a snap and looked toward the figure of the guard now coming purposefully toward him. At once the hated and well-remembered scent of the man filled the stallion's nostrils. He did not run from the man as he might have from another. Instead the tiny ears flattened against his skull, his big eyes blazed and he leaped forward rearing on his hind legs. Before the guard could stop and turn Khala Hawa was upon him. The forehoofs drove down only once, and the man fell to the ground never to rise again. Now the panic which is always close to every horse took hold of the big stallion. The hated smell of an enemy was in his nostrils, the urge to be with his beloved master was in his mind and about him were the unfamiliar surroundings which were part of the painful happenings of the day. With a shrill scream the supple animal leaped far over the fallen slaver and driving hard, Khala Hawa headed for the open desert. Running with the speed which had earned him his name, Khala Hawa, wind of the desert, the grey stallion drove in a great circle until with the instinct of the wild things he set his course unerringly for the camp of Akim Abou where he was sure he would find the gentle fingers and a tid-bit of grain to tickle his palate.

Chapter 11

HASSAN WAS RIGHT, the men of the Bedouin would not be fooled for long. Barely had they entered the town when they realized they had been tricked. At once with Akim Abou in their lead they streaked for the home camp in the foothills, driving their camels unmercifully. By the time they reached the camp the older ones who still survived had bandaged their wounds, and with the fatalism of those who live in the desert they were busily doing what they could to restore order. It was they who described to Akim Abou what had happened.

At once the Sheik sent men to scout for the trail left by the raiders. The scouts returned one by one to report failure. Hassan had done his work well and no track was left in the sand for the Bedouin to follow. Akim Abou called his men together for a council of war, and many suggestions were made, discussed and discarded. Gloom descended on them all, for they, more than anyone else knew the futility of searching the broad expanses of the desert. Often had they raided an enemy camp suddenly, and as suddenly disappeared into the desert wiping away their trail just as Hassan's men had done. Gladly would they have fought a foe which outnumbered them ten to one, but now they could not even hunt for the foe. Silence fell on the assembly and no one sought to break it. It was while they sat silently each man busy with his unhappy thoughts that the shrill scream of a stallion called across the sands to them. Each man involuntarily lifted his head. It was Emal Dukka, Khala Hawa's old enemy but long since his friend, who broke the silence.

"The wild horse. Why does he call?"

Another man, one of those who had been sent to count the horses in the herd, spoke up.

"The stallion of the boy Saya? He was not in the herd when I counted. It was my thought that he was frightened by the raid and ran away."

The men looked from one to another. Even in this

tragic hour the actions of a horse were important to them. Silently they agreed with the herdsman's guess at Khala Hawa's actions.

The drumming of the great horse's hoofs came to them now, and as they looked in the direction of the sound, the powerful body of the grey stallion lunged over the crest of the dune and bore down on the camp. The eyes of the men filled with admiration, for the noble animal ran with the grace and speed of a gazelle. But the practised eye of Akim Abou told him something was wrong. Quickly he sent a man to catch up the horse and lead it to their council circle. Then, holding the heavy rope which still dragged from the stallion's neck, he spoke to his men.

"Look you," he said. "This is no rope from our camp. Further I can tell you that no rope ever would hold this horse. He was held by his love for my son."

The men murmured to each other and nodded, for they knew this to be true. But one man spoke up.

"Then the horse was stolen in the raid," he commented. "This rope then means the horse has freed himself. But it does not help us. See how the horse is lathered. He has run many miles. This proves only that our foe is far away."

But Akim Abou was not to be put off, for he was sure he read the signs correctly. His voice urged them as he said:

"That is not true. Look you. The horse has escaped, that is certain. Furthermore, this horse would not have returned had my son been at his side. The lather on his sides means that he has run fast, not far."

Emil Dukka spoke now.

"Your words may be true, Akim Abou. But I do not understand how this can help us."

Then Akim Abou uttered the words which sent the men springing to their feet.

"Men of the Bedouin I tell you this. Khala Hawa has been in the raiders' camp. He has escaped from that camp. The raiders wiped out their trail, that we know. But look you. The wind has died out for the evening. One horse running in the sand leaves a track which can be followed at a gallop in the moonlight. Your war-mares men! We back-track the trail Khala Hawa has given us! It will lead us to the raiders!"

A single great shout went up from two hundred throats and then the men of the Bedouin ran for their mounts. Minutes later a wild horde roared across the desert. Caught in the excitement the great grey stallion ran with them, and effortlessly he ran alongside the mare Baku who carried on her back Akim Abou, father of his beloved Saya.

Chapter 12

THE BEDOUIN RESORTED to no tricks. They did not skulk in the shadows until the time was convenient. They did not try to hide their coming because, in their anger, they wanted only to close with the enemy and avenge their dead. This time their foolhardiness was their advantage. So swiftly did they come, so wild was their attack that hardly had the sound of their coming awakened the sleeping raiders than the men of Akim Abou were among them. Swords and daggers flashed silver in the moonlight, and a few moments later the silver changed to bright scarlet. Long rifles spat

bursts of flame brighter than the tiny fires still winking here and there in the camp.

In the heat of the battle nothing could be done for the slaves who were chained in the long line. But the many who had been taken from the line to act as servants were bound for the night with rope. As these were discovered in the fight, they were quickly freed with a knife slash. One freed early in the fight was Saya, and with a hasty prayer to Allah the boy picked up a rifle from the dead hand of a fallen raider and joined in the battle. And as the boy joined his father's men his voice rose with them in the shout:

"Allah il Allah. There is no God but Allah."

Maddened with excitement, Khala Hawa plunged about in the fighting. Seeking he knew not what his powerful grey body hurtled through the milling tangle of men. Then his sensitive ears picked out a familiar voice, and with a high whinny of pleasure he dashed in the direction of the sound. Saya saw him coming and now it was the boy's turn to cry out with delight.

"Khala Hawa! My great horse! Stand. Stand."

Now the long and sometimes tedious hours which the boy had spent in training the horse paid their due. Still as a statue, disregarding the maelstrom about him, Khala Hawa waited. Only when Saya had vaulted to his back, and touched his heels lightly to the great animal's side did the stallion galvanize into life. Catching up the still trailing rope, Saya guided the horse with the makeshift rein on the side of the sleek grey neck, and his slim brown legs against the horse's side. Into the fight they went, and both had a big score to settle with the slavers.

It must be said here that the horse was the better warrior of the two, though it was Saya who did the thinking for both. The shining black hoofs of Khala Hawa accounted for many of the raiders that night and Saya's rifle ended the careers of more of them.

Dawn broke to see the end of the fighting. Those of the raiders who were able caught up mounts and, fighting off the Bedouin as best they could, escaped into the desert. Drooping with fatigue Saya looked about him and saw no one left to fight. He let the rifle drop to the ground, and for a moment he rested against the massive neck of his horse. Then reining the tired stallion about, he lifted the rein in signal to return to the main camp where already a little knot of Bedouins were beginning to gather. So tired was he that Saya did not even hear the high whine of the ricocheting bullet, nor the dull thud as it struck. He was aware of what happened only when Khala Hawa with a high scream gave a great bound which tumbled the boy to the ground. He jumped to his feet to see the stallion stretched out on the ground, blood gushing from a great wound in his body. A cry of horror and anguish broke from Saya's lips even as he turned to dash to the spring for a handful of mud to stanch the red flow which was so quickly spilling Khala Hawa's life out upon the sand.

Chapter 13

FOR THE MOST PART the little oasis was silent even though several hundred men, women and children were there. The Bedouin had won a decisive victory over the raiders, and while this should have been an occasion of rejoicing it was instead one of great solemnity. Nearly every family from the camp of Akim Abou had lost at least one loved member. Besides those who had fallen never to rise again many a man had been brought down by a bullet, and it would be long before these would tend the flocks, or urge a camel across the desert.

A wild nomadic life in the grim desert leaves little time for useless grieving, and the Bedouin went about their work and kept their sorrows to themselves. Food must be prepared. Wounds must be bandaged. Water must be brought from the tiny spring which gave up its precious fluid in small quantities. And so the Bedouin, as would the other wild ones of the desert, licked their wounds and faced the future.

Perhaps the quietest of all those in the oasis, was the little knot of people gathered around Saya and his fallen horse. Akim Abou, his wife Corza and little Nedda were there but they did not interfere. Many of the tribe's bravest warriors were there also, for that day Saya and his great stallion had earned a new respect from them. They watched carefully as Saya worked on the great wound in the horse's side. Again and again Saya repacked it with fresh mud to stanch the bleeding, pressing as he did so, with his fingers against the great pulsing arteries. But these men were practical horsemen, and they looked at each other and slowly shook their heads. To each of them a fine horse was like a brother and their eyes saddened as they realized the great stallion must go. They murmured softly to each other.

"The wound is bad. The horse cannot live."

"Better a merciful bullet. The horse suffers much."

"The bullet has torn vitals. Inside he bleeds as well."

"A curse is on our camp that the great grey one

must die. His colts would have been famous across Arabia."

"Tell the boy he wastes his time. We must return to our camp."

Saya heard none of their voices. His own heart was aching with the fear that this time his beautiful animal was brought to its death. Khala Hawa lay without moving, his great eyes closed, and only the slight rise and fall of the massive chest admitted that life still lingered. Finally Saya paused in his effort, and rested, mute with fatigue which wracked his body. His father came to him and dropping to his knees put his muscular arm about the boy's shoulders. He spoke softly:

"My son it sorrows me to speak thus to thee. Thy horse has already entered the vale of shadows and from here there is no returning. Join thy mother and thy sister boy, and let me with my rifle put a merciful end to the suffering of a brave warrior."

Saya did not raise his head for a moment but when he did a little smile played around the corners of his lips. His voice was low also as he answered his father, but it was firm.

"Khala Hawa is not yet dead, my father. So it is with the Bedouin. We do not bury him until he dies."

Akim Abou looked down at his son as the boy phrased the old expression. He started to answer, but decided to remain silent. He knew the great love which had grown between the boy and his horse and he knew that Saya would stay with the stallion until the mighty lungs drew their last breath. He reflected that this was as it should be for Khala Hawa would never have deserted the boy. Now the Sheik rose to his feet and with a wave of his hand called away those who watched. He took Saya's mother by the hand with a whispered word sent her with Nedda to prepare for the journey home. Quietly he directed men to erect one of the broad low goat-hair tents over the fallen horse and the boy who attended it. Then he placed in the tent a rifle and ammunition, a supply of food and a well-filled skin of water. Sheik Akim Abou had done all he could for his son, and now with a last look at the boy, he turned and directed his people to form a caravan for the trip home.

Saya was hardly aware of the attentions he received. He looked up as the tent was erected and nodded his appreciation at the cool semi-darkness which closed out the blinding rays of the sun from his wounded horse. From the skin of water he wet a cloth and moistened the lips of the horse which were beginning to parch with the fever already setting in. Now Saya stood and walked out of the tent. He waved to the caravan as it left the oasis. The Bedouin with Akim Abou at their head were going home. He went to the spring and cut a small quantity of the grass which grew there and brought it to the tent, hoping that Khala Hawa would awaken and find himself hungry.

Now the boy examined the dreadful wound again, wet the fever-thickened lips of the horse, then with no thought for himself he laid down beside the great horse and slept.

The sun was already high when Saya awakened and jumped to his feet with a guilty start. But his haste seemed wasted for Khala Hawa lay as though dead. He ran to the horse, dropped to his knees and put his ear to the massive chest. A sigh of relief escaped him. Though it was faint, Saya could distinctly hear the low rumble of the once powerful heart. His own heart ached for though he had stopped the bleeding, Saya knew that the horse had bled internally as well. He knew also that vital organs may have been injured beyond repair. Saya sat quietly a moment thinking. He remembered the other bullet which had brought Khala Hawa down and how his exploring fingers in the wound had found the bullet flattened and misshapen against the rib. But this time there was no rib to flatten the bullet and halt its course. This time the bullet had penetrated deeply. Even now perhaps, resting in the vitals of Khala Hawa, the missile halted the processes of healing.

Saya, son of the desert, knew nothing of medicine as we know it, but he did have the wisdom of the wild people, gathered through thousands of years of wandering their wasteland. Then he remembered watching his father attend a horse which had been shot. He remembered what his father had done and quickly he made up his mind. He went again to the spring and from a small clump of reeds growing there, he selected one of the strongest. Carefully, using his sharp knife the boy peeled it. He did not let his hand touch the peeled portion and though he could not have told you why he did this, he knew with the instinct of the desert man that nature had kept the reed free from all source of contamination under the bark. Now with his knife, and still not touching the peeled portion, he carefully split the reed three quarters of its length. He carefully inserted a tiny wedge of wood at the top of the split thus holding the split wide open. Now, by grasping the unsplit portion of the reed, and pressing just below the wedge of wood, Saya had a rough but very workable tweezers several inches long.

The boy returned to the horse's side and sat down on the ground beside it. For a long time he sat there as though considering exactly what he should do. Then, he thrust his chin forward and with a look of determination he began his task. Carefully he cleaned the mud from the wound, noting with satisfaction that it no longer bled. Now he prepared for his next move. His eyes went Heavenward, and a silent prayer to Allah crossed his mind. Then as though further delay would weaken his determination, Saya closed the rough tweezers and set about his work.

Carefully but firmly he sent the reed searching into the wound for the hidden bullet. The fine horse groaned and moved his powerful body as the pain of the operation penetrated even to his inner consciousness. But Saya persisted for he well knew that his friend and companion was near to death. If his homely surgery should hasten that death, very well. It was the will of Allah that he try his best to save Khala Hawa. Beyond what help he could give, only a miracle could save the horse.

Suddenly Saya's home-made surgical instrument struck a hard object. It could be nothing but the bullet. He relaxed his grip on the reed and felt the ends open under his fingers. Slowly he sent the probe into the wound a fraction further, and when he again compressed it to close the ends, a hard object resisted. Holding firmly Saya drew back on the probe. Again and again the ends of his tweezer snapped together as the object was lost to his grip. Again and again he recovered it, lost it, recovered it again until finally, shaking with nervousness he drew out the flattened and discolored bullet. Again the lifeblood poured out on the sand, bubbling high from the terrible wound, but this time Saya did not stanch it at once. He knew well the cleansing effect it would have. He watched closely however, and presently the flow stopped.

Saya heaved a sigh of relief and placed his ear to the horse's chest. A low thump-thump in steady rhythm came to his ear. Khala Hawa was indeed in the vale of shadow, but also, as Saya had said, he was not yet dead. Saya rose wearily knowing that for the time being the fight was with the grey horse, that he himself had done all he could. Conscious of a nagging hunger, for he had eaten little in two days Saya turned to the parcel of food. As he opened it, Saya uttered a little cry of delight, for in addition to the food Saya's mother had put in a small package of healing herbs, which had been found in the supplies of the raiders. Saya lost no time in starting a fire, and in a few moments two cooking pots bubbled cheerfully. One contained savory mutton, the other boiled water from the spring to make, with the herbs, a healing poultice for Khala Hawa's wound.

The boy ate his fill quickly and returned to the horse which lay so quietly on the floor of the tent. Using the water and the herbs he made a poultice and carefully packed the wound, spreading a torn strip of cloth over it to keep away the dirt and flies which buzzed in the tent. But Saya shook his head. He knew that the strength of the horse, tremendous though it had been, was nearly drained. Only food could bring it back but with Khala Hawa lying in a stupor how could he be made to eat? Back to the fire went Saya, and again he took the pot of boiling water. Now with barley he made a thick gruel. Some of his precious salt went into the pot, and then Saya set it aside to cool, while he returned to the spring for a fresh supply of water.

Now he went to the horse again and sat down cross-legged at its head. Though it took all his strength, he forced the horse's head up from the sand, and inched himself forward until it rested in his lap. Now Saya performed a difficult task. Holding the lips of the horse open, he forced bits of gruel between them, and with a few drops of water from the sheep-skin container, he managed to slide the bits of gruel down the horse's throat. Patiently, though his arms ached with the strain the boy continued to force the tiny bits of gruel into the horse's mouth. It was slow and wearying work. Much of the gruel dropped to the ground to be quickly absorbed by the ever-hungry sand. Finally the last bit was gone and the tired boy rose to let the stallion's head settle back against the sand. Saya had tried his best, but he knew that the tiny bit of food which reached the horse's stomach would throw little weight into the balance on which the beautiful horse's life hung.

Saya's work took many hours to accomplish. Sundown came before he finished his meager meal of mutton, and his head was nodding over the still half-full pot of food. He put it aside and, hardly realizing what he did, went to Khala Hawa and put his head down to the horse's chest to listen to the heart beat. This time he heard nothing, nor was he concerned. As his head touched the sleek side of the recumbent horse, Saya fell soundly asleep. Disturbed by the weight of the boy's head Khala Hawa's great head lifted from the sand and turned so that the wide nostrils touched the boy's face softly. Contented that his little friend was at his side, the big horse let his head drop back to the sand, for his strength was so lacking that holding his head up was more effort than he could make. The desert night came on again and horse and boy slept peacefully. Perhaps Allah looked down from his high place and spread a shield of protection over them, for no danger came to them that night.

Chapter 14

NEDDA AND HER FATHER sat quietly on the goatskin rug while Corza served the evening meal. When the mother dropped to the rug also they picked up their food bowls and made a pretense of eating. But none of them was hungry. It was strange to sit there eating with the place of Saya empty. Three nights had passed now while the boy was alone in the desert with his dying horse. Akim Abou kept his face impassive for the philosophy of the Bedouin forbade that he show emotion. His son was now to be considered nearly a man, and a man's work must be done. That Saya chose to stay with his wounded horse had Akim Abou's approval. Often had he stayed beside a wounded animal in just this way, day after day, night after night, attending to its needs nursing it through its pain until finally the horse either returned to good health, or as Allah dictated, died. Secretly, he worried over Saya and he had already determined that when enough days went past to see Saya's food supply diminished, he would go himself to find his son and bring him safely home.

It was different with women. Corza showed plainly in her face that Saya's continued absence worried her. Little Nedda sniffled from time to time, so close was she to tears. Then Corza broke the silence.

"Husband," she said. "My heart is fearful. Our son should not have been left alone."

Akim Abou looked kindly at her: "This is the way of our world, wife. Could I say to my son, "leave this one who is thy best friend to die alone?"

"But my father," Nedda spoke up. "Men should have been left with him. He is a boy only."

Akim Abou smiled at his little daughter and spoke gently for he was very fond of the sweet little girl.

"Little one, how could I say to this man or that one 'Leave thy family on the desert and stay to protect this one of mine?' No this I could not do. Nor could I stay myself to protect him for I am Sheik of our tribe and to me our people look for leadership. No little one, it is the way of the world that the needs of the one must give way to the needs of the many."

Now Corza spoke.

"You are right my husband. Though it is small solace to a mother. Saya could not leave his friend, nor could you command another to stay with him."

She sighed softly and reconciled herself to the ways of the world in which she lived.

"If only he were not alone," she said. "If one has another to speak with, at least he is spared the facing of danger alone." Now she turned to Nedda. "Come little one. Thy bed calls to thee."

Nedda arose obediently and followed her mother to the back of the tent which was draped to form the sleeping quarters. She submitted to going to bed but lay thoughtfully staring at the ceiling of the black tent. Her eyes were round with the idea which was slowly forming in her mind. She heard her mother and father find their sleeping robes and when their regular breathing told her they were asleep she rose from her bed and so softly did she move that not a whisper of sound was heard. Nedda stole quietly out of the tent into the darkness.

No moon shone but the faint silvery light from the stars was enough for this desert-bred girl to find her way to the pasture. Her lips pursed in the low whistle which Saya had taught her and immediately an answering whinny came from the darkness. In a few moments the beautiful Ja Mi Li loomed before her. The mare dropped her head low so that the tiny hands of Nedda could reach it. Now the mare nuzzled the little girl's garments for the taste of food which Saya usually brought her. It was forthcoming, for long since the little girl had formed the habit of keeping a handful of dates, or a tiny bit of barley in the folds of her garments. Then the little girl, in the way of children, spoke to the horse as though it were another person.

"I am fearful, Ja Mi Li," she said. "Saya does not come home, nor does Khala Hawa. My father says that they are safe and that probably no harm will come to them. But my mother says it is not happy to face danger alone. Do you think we should go to them?"

Ja Mi Li pricked up her ears at the mention of the familiar name-sounds and nickered softly, but beyond that her limited intelligence could not direct her. However, the nervousness of the girl transmitted itself to her and she stamped a small hoof impatiently. Then Nedda made up her mind. With some difficulty she clambered to the back of Ja Mi Li and urged the horse forward. The trail of the returning Bedouin was heavy and, no effort having been made to conceal it, the track remained only slightly smoothed by the winds. Holding firmly to a tuft of the mare's mane, Nedda guided her to this trail and set her upon it, but the mare was heavily in foal and the little girl tried to hold her to a slow pace. But the excitement of these unusual happenings had taken hold of Ja Mi Li and ignoring the restraining hands of the little girl the mare broke into a long easy lope which would eat up the desert miles. Realizing that the mare would correctly gauge her own strength, Nedda simply clung on, and soon was enjoying the exhilarating ride. Nor did she even bother to guide the mare for as horses will, Ja Mi Li understood at once that the old trail of the Bedouin was the road to follow, and without faltering in her long easy stride she whirled through the night.

Hour after hour they travelled until finally, silhouetted against the faint light, the palms of the little oasis loomed ahead. It was not difficult to locate the darker blob of Saya's tent. Nedda slid down from Ja Mi Li in front of the shelter, threw back the flap and entered. Ja Mi Li unhesitatingly followed, lowering her head nearly to the ground to follow the girl into the squat shelter. They found Saya fast asleep, his head pillowed on the great chest of Khala Hawa. The grey stallion slept also. Ja Mi Li sniffed once at the body of the stallion and once at the sleeping boy, then with a sigh of contentment, she folded her legs under her and laid down on the still warm sand.

Nedda's first impulse was to awaken her brother, but instead she felt about in the dark tent until she found sleeping robes. She rolled up in them and was soon fast asleep.

Chapter 15

THE SLANTING rays of the sun, barely clearing a distant sand dune, shone through the tent flap which Nedda had failed to drop. They pierced the closed eyelids of Saya and forced them open. The boy raised his head from the sleek chest of Khala Hawa and looked around in some puzzlement. He was in a tent which was as it should be, but it was not the home tent. The boy stood up and looked around him. Here was the beautiful dark creamy body of Ja Mi Li sound asleep, her sides bulging with the colt soon to be born, and here was his little sister, Nedda, equally soundly asleep.

Saya smiled for the first time in days, then sobered at the thought of these added responsibilities. Then he thought of his horse. Quickly he went to Khala Hawa's side and pressed his ear to the powerful chest. Khala Hawa's flaring nostrils fluttered but, reassured at the familiar scent, he made no unnecessary move, for instinct dictated that he preserve his strength. A slow but regular pounding inside the great chest cavern comforted Saya, and now he stood to look about him and survey his situation.

Two more charges had been sent to him by Allah, his little sister and the beautiful mare, Ja Mi Li. Then his eye, practised by a life with horses, saw something. Quickly he walked to the mare, who still lay on the warm sand sound asleep. Her breathing was irregular, her sides heaved, and a thin dark line along her flanks told him that even while she slept her discomfort lathered her body slightly. No, not two more charges had been sent to him, but three. For soon Ja Mi Li would bring her foal into the world. The mare lifted her head and looked wildly about. She saw Saya standing close to her, his eyes following her every movement. In him she recognized a friend. She lunged to her feet and immediately thrust her sleek head into his hands. A soft whimpering sound came from her throat, and in this greatest of moments, the beautiful mare turned to the boy.

As always, Saya was ready with a quiet word and a

firm, gentle hand. He led the mare to the very center of the tent then, with an encouraging word uttered in his low assured voice, he put his hand on her satiny nose. It was more of a caress than a command, but after a few moments, Ja Mi Li yielded and sank gratefully down to the ground. Now her fears were gone, and her instinct told her what was to happen. Already she was preparing to face a new life, a life in which she would shield her colt from harm with all her strength. It was during this little drama that Nedda awakened and watched with wonderment. She saw the frightened mare calm under the gentle hand of her brother, and she saw her sink passively to rest on the ground. Nedda knew something important was about to happen, but she dared not interrupt. Now as Ja Mi Li stretched on the floor of the tent, she came to her brother and spoke:

"Saya, what happens? Are you angry at us for coming?"

Saya turned quickly and smiled at his little sister.

"I am not angry, little sister, that you came. Though it is bad. You should not have come."

"But why?" Nedda asked. "Mother said the worst of your waiting here was loneliness. If you only had someone to talk with. . . ."

Saya interrupted but not angrily, for though his problems were multiplied, he could not be angry with this sweet little one who looked so often to him for his wisdom in many things. He nodded towards the mare.

"It is nice to speak with thee, little sister, but now we have no time to speak."

He waved his arm around the tent.

"We are four now, Khala Hawa, Ja Mi Li, yourself and myself."

Then he nodded again towards the beautiful mare and added:

"Soon we will be five. Ja Mi Li will bear her colt within the hour. We must hurry to help her should she need our help."

Nedda's already large eyes grew huge and round, and she did not pause to question, but when Saya sent her to the spring for water, she scurried as fast as her plump little legs would carry her. Meanwhile, Saya rekindled his fire. Soon a pot of water was heating over the low flame, and a pot of barley gruel warmed also. Though Saya knew that his immediate attention must go to Ja Mi Li, he had time to care for his great stallion also. He tore his burnoose to make soft cloths should they be needed, adjusted the water pot so that the water would stay warm but not too hot, and now he could only wait. Meanwhile, there was Khala Hawa. He spoke to Nedda.

"Little sister, you will watch the mare. See . . .

she rests easily, but soon she will be disturbed. I will attend Khala Hawa meanwhile. You watch with Ja Mi Li."

Nedda nodded soberly but eagerly.

"Must I be quiet?" she asked.

Saya smiled at her.

"No, of course not. We can talk. It will not hurt."

Now he went to Khala Hawa. Again he listened to the great heart of the noble horse. Though the stallion lay quietly, a reassuring thump of his heart could be heard. Moreover, the thump was not erratic but regular. Saya was encouraged. Again he forced the tiny bits of gruel into Khala Hawa's mouth and washed them down the horse's throat with sips of water. It was small fare for a horse whose powerful body demanded much green grass, but as Saya hoped, it might help to stem the tide which drained the strength of the stallion. Then Nedda called to him.

"Saya! Ja Mi Li acts strangely. Come quickly!"

He hurried to his sister's side and with practised eye looked at the mare. He knew at once that her time had come. A speck of froth had appeared at the corners of Ja Mi Li's mouth, and a light coating of lather gathered in the hollows of her flanks.

Nedda was frightened.

"Is there nothing we can do, Saya? You are so wise! What must we do?"

Saya laid a restraining hand on her arm.

"We must only wait, Nedda. Ja Mi Li is wiser than we are. Only if trouble besets her must we interfere."

As they waited and watched, the wonder of creation opened to them. The little colt emerged from its mother's body, curled up and encased in the nearly transparent envelope. They saw Ja Mi Li, acting by instinct, lift her head, bare her sharp teeth and tear open the envelope to give her baby the now much-needed air. They heard the whimper of the new-born colt and they knew that all was right. Now Saya decided to act, for while Ja Mi Li could have gone on without their help, there was no need to call further upon her diminished strength. While Nedda laved the sweaty head of the mare and cleaned her flanks with cool water, Saya washed the colt carefully. It whimpered at his attention but because it had not yet stood upon its legs, it was helpless to resist. Saya smiled at it knowing that in another few hours it would be a wild thing, able to run beside its mother at an amazing speed should danger threaten. Now Saya took hold of Ja Mi Li's bridle and urged her to her feet. Turning, he put his arms about the thin chest of the colt and with a great heave stood it upon its wobbly legs. Stumbling with it as it faltered uncertainly Saya coaxed it to its mother's side and then he joined Nedda to stand with her laughing in glee as the colt nursed.

Nedda chortled: "Saya, Ja Mi Li's foal is a colt! Are you not happy?"

But Saya only nodded. Long since he had been sure this would happen.

"Think you," he said importantly. "That my great Khala Hawa would fail to have a son to succeed him? Did my father fail to have a son? Indeed not. Look at me!"

Nedda looked at him obediently but as she often looked at him anyway she merely nodded agreeably. Sometimes it was hard for her to understand this big brother of hers but always it was fun to be with him. So that which she failed to comprehend, she simply overlooked.

But now, Saya, desert-reared and wise in the ways of survival went to work in earnest. He placed the loaded rifle handily and told Nedda to fire it should danger threaten. He well knew that his sister, young as she was, knew how a rifle should be fired though she had no training as a marksman. Now he ranged with his knife in hand, the length and breadth of the oasis, cutting the longer tufts of grass and piling them in his worn burnoose to be carried back to camp. Ja Mi Li must be fed so that her milk would flow heavily to give strength to her new son, but she could not be allowed to roam at will. Again and again he filled his burnoose trudging back to the tent to drop the grass in the center. Soon the pile was high with tender grass and Ja Mi Li was free to nibble whenever she chose.

When the battle with the raiders had ended, the

Bedouins had quickly buried the enemy dead under the sands of the desert. Then combing the oasis they took the supplies left by the raiders, for these are the legitimate rewards of a desert war. Many fine guns and supplies of ammunition were taken, and food, robes, knives and swords. And all were of good quality. However the fight had spread over the entire oasis and as Saya went into every nook and cranny in his search for grass, he found three rifles which had been dropped in such a way as to be concealed from the eyes of Akim Abou's men. These he took joyfully back to camp.

As soon as he returned to their camp, Saya had to load each one and demonstrate his skill as a rifleman to Nedda. But now he cleaned the guns, loaded them and placed them carefully in the tent.

"Ahee little sister there is still much work to be done."

Nedda nodded solemnly and asked, "What can I do?"

Saya nodded toward Khala Hawa who still lay quietly with only a sobbing breath to prove that he lived. The rise and fall of his great chest was so slight that it could scarcely be noticed.

"I must do more for Khala Hawa. His strength does not return and thus far I have given him little food."

Nedda looked at the horse and shook her head slowly as she answered.

"I heard our father and the men speaking. They said you wasted your effort. They said no horse could live from such a wound as Khala Hawa received."

Saya's voice was tired as he answered.

"It may be that they are right, little sister. It is a great wound."

Then the boy's head lifted and his face was determined.

"He is a great horse. No other horse has the courage of my Khala Hawa. And more, Nedda! He has a great desire to live."

Again, the wisdom of horsemen through the ages which was instilled in the Bedouin boy was apparent as he spoke.

"To many horses life is a burden. They must carry loads which are too heavy for them. They are given little and poor food. As the years go by these horses weary of life as do men who are overburdened. When the opportunity comes these horses die quickly."

Nedda's eyes grew round as she listened to her brother. The boy went on.

"My Khala Hawa is like to a man who has lived a lusty, happy life, a life of strength and fire! He does not want to die. He wants to live, to run with me over the sand dunes again. On this strength of heart I count heavily, though the strength of his body is all but gone."

As though in answer to the boy's fervent speech a

long shuddering sigh escaped Khala Hawa's throat and the great head lifted slightly from the sand only to settle back at once. The movement brought Saya to his feet.

"See Nedda," he cried. "It is as I said. Look you! His strength is all but gone, yet he tries. He tries!"

Now Saya hurried to the pot over the fire which he had filled with gruel and placed there to warm. He had Nedda to help him now and he determined to give his beloved horse every aid he could. He spoke wisely to his sister again.

"Food is strength Nedda. Khala Hawa cannot eat, but I have forced a small amount of gruel into his stomach. Come, help me. Perhaps together we can give him strength."

Saya took robes and rolled them into compact bundles. Taking them to the prostrate stallion, he lifted its muzzle until it pointed upward. Then as Saya directed, Nedda placed the blanket rolls beneath the horse's head to hold it in that position. Now handing the pot of gruel to Nedda, Saya went to work.

Now Saya inserted a clean stick into the side of the horse's mouth, and lightly touched the roof with the tip. At once Khala Hawa's mouth opened and Saya was ready. Already he had prepared two smooth, slender blocks of wood. These he set into each side of the horse's mouth to prop it open. Now the boy passed a light cord around the lower jaw and over the tongue, for in Khala Hawa's semi-conscious state the tongue itself could be swallowed and the fine animal choked to death thereby.

The rest was easy. With Nedda to drop the bits of gruel into the open mouth of the horse, and Saya to flush the strength-giving food down the open red throat, they soon had the pot emptied. And this time a goodly portion of food went to strengthen the weakened horse. Khala Hawa stirred uneasily once or twice for this was hardly the natural manner for a horse to eat his meal. But involuntarily the stallion swallowed the food, and finally Saya removed the cords and the blocks of wood to let the horse's mouth close comfortably. Then they took away the blanket rolls and Khala Hawa's head dropped wearily to the sand. Again Saya put his ear to the sleek grey chest and listened to the slow thumping of the great heart. His eyes lost their tired look for a moment because it seemed to the boy that already the beat of the heart was stronger. Then his own heart sank again as he cleansed the great wound. A terrible injury had come to the beautiful creature, and despite his fine work death might still come.

Now their little camp settled down for the night. Ja Mi Li shouldered her new son aside, and went to feed at the pile of cut grass. When her appetite was satisfied she turned again to the tiny horse and coaxed it to nurse. His hunger satisfied, the colt folded his tired, spindly legs and laid down to sleep. Ja Mi Li went over the little one carefully, then, satisfied that all was well with him she laid down also for a much needed rest.

Now Saya and Nedda turned their attention to themselves. Quickly the pot of mutton was warmed and with cool sweet water from the spring the boy and girl made their simple meal. Too weary to think further they found their robes and settled down quietly for the night. So quickly did they fall asleep that neither of them heard the thin wail which arose from the desert many miles away. Long and mournful it rang out echoing back and forth among the dunes. The jackal pack was on the hunt and the wind blowing toward them brought with it the scent of a nearly-dead stallion, a weary mare and a new-born colt.

The hated man-scent was there also, but so faint it was not to be feared.

Chapter 16

SAYA DID NOT know what awakened him. He only knew that one moment he was lost in a pleasant dream wherein he and Khala Hawa, miraculously whole again, galloped across the smooth desert sand. The next moment, he was awake and straining to hear a sound in the vast silence of the desert. When no sound came, he quietly slipped out of his robes and walked across the tent to stir the fire and put more wood upon it. As the flames leaped up, he looked about. Nedda lay quietly in her robes. The colt stretched at full length slept soundly, and only his silky little nose twitched at the tickling of the sand from the ground. Ja Mi Li lay quietly as did Khala Hawa, but both were awake, and Saya noted in surprise that the ears of both of them were held forward to listen as he did himself.

The boy was puzzled, but as he walked to the entrance of the tent to look about the camp, his puzzlement was dispelled by a long quavering howl which pierced the desert stillness with devilish menace. Jackals! The boy's face whitened, for at once he knew the meaning of that howl. Well he knew that the scent of the three partially helpless horses had carried to the pack. Saya knew, too, that there would be a pack, for the jackal is an arrant coward and he does not run alone. But the boy was worried and with reason. He was aware that they were camped fairly close to the big feeding grounds in the foothills where thousands of sheep, goats, horses and camels grazed. In this area, the jackal packs were large, and the pack which was coming toward their camp was bound to be a big one. But not for a moment did Saya think to run with

Nedda to a place of safety. He it was in whom the beautiful mare and the magnificent stallion had placed their trust, and Ja Mi Li, in addition, looked to the boy for the protection of her new colt. It did not even enter the boy's mind to violate that trust. Instead, his thoughts turned at once to the most practical way in which to defend their camp when the pack came, and the jackal pack would come! Of that he was certain.

Quickly now he ran to his little sister's side.

"Nedda!" he urged. "Nedda! Wake up!"

Sleepily the little girl opened her eyes. Then she awakened completely and slid from beneath her robe like a little wild thing. She did not speak, for Saya's cautious whisper suggested danger to her, and an incautious voice can sometimes bring a raiding party down upon a camp. Saya explained quickly.

"A jackal pack," he said. "And the wind is blowing from us towards the place from where the cry came. They've scented the horses. You must help me prepare so that we can fight them off."

Nedda allowed herself a short moment of fear, and a tiny sob escaped her throat, for she, like all children of the desert, had learned the danger of the jackal pack. Then she settled down to work as Saya directed her.

"Quickly," he said. "The tent must come down."

Tugging at the pegs which held the goat-hair tent,

they struck it, rolled it up and pushed it far to one side so that it would not become an obstacle over which to stumble in the heat of battle. More wood and dried camel dung were gathered hastily from the plentiful supply left by the raiders, and new fires were built; four of them forming a square with the horses in the middle. The leaping flames illuminated a considerable area about the camp, thus making it difficult for a skulking beast to draw near without being seen. Next, Saya moved the cooking fire to the center of the square and placed near it spare fuel and several long sticks of wood. One of the long sticks he thrust into the fire so that only the end caught the blaze. Now, he turned to his sister and bade her sit on the ground near the center fire. Quickly he ran to the place where his rifles lay. Now he was glad to have the three beautiful weapons he had found. With these and his father's rifle, which Akim Abou had left with him, he was well armed. The rifle of the Bedouin was long of barrel with a handsomely carved stock, beautifully inlaid with gold and ivory. But the weapon was a single shot. Therein lay the basis of Saya's defense plan. Bringing the guns to Nedda's side, he sat down beside her and carefully taught her to load the weapons. Firearms were a common thing in the girl's life, and though she had few occasions to handle one, except perhaps to fetch her father's weapon for him, she was familiar with them. Her little hands were nimble, and in a few moments she had learned to load the rifles as quickly and as well as Saya himself.

Now Saya arose and looked carefully about him. Again and again as he worked, he peered toward the edge of the oasis in all directions, but he had seen nothing. However, the wild, mournful howl of the jackals had rung out over the desert more and more often, and each time a wail was heard, Saya knew the pack to be closer. But now he was ready. He walked back to Nedda, selected a rifle and placed it in the crook of his arm. He listened carefully to one long howl, and this time he did not sit down.

"We are ready, Nedda," he said. "More I cannot do."

Nedda nodded soberly. "I am not afraid, Saya."

Saya smiled a little crooked smile at her. She was afraid, and Saya knew it, for he himself was afraid. But long since his father had told him something. Akim Abou had said:

"My son, do not be ashamed of fear. Be only ashamed of cowardice. The man who tells you that he has never been afraid is either a fool or a liar. Fear can be conquered. Despite your fear, force yourself to act with courage. This, my son, is the way of a truly brave man."

The thought comforted Saya for, though he knew he was afraid, something within told him that he would defend his little sister and his animals to his last breath. Again the call of the jackal came to him, and this time it was quite near. Now the scent of the horses must have been strong in the nostrils of the skulking beasts for, as though this one call had been a signal, an answering call went up from twenty throats. Saya started when he heard the chorus because at last he had a means of estimating the size of the pack, and with a sinking heart he realized that no bigger pack of jackals had ever coursed the desert. Turning to Nedda, he spoke:

"Little sister," he said, "Soon they come. Look you. See the firebrand thrust into the fire so that only the end burns?"

Nedda nodded, and Saya went on.

"Should a jackal break through our ring of fire, seize the brand and thrust it in his face. He will leave you quickly."

Nedda accepted this wisdom and felt some comfort that she also should have a weapon of sorts, but she asked:

"You will not leave me, Saya? You will not move far away when the pack comes?"

He quickly reassured her. "I will stand right here to shoot, for how else can I take the fresh rifles after you load them? No, I will be close to you, Nedda." He paused for a moment, then, his face serious, he went on: "We have done our best, Nedda. Now we must wait for the pack to come and then fight well. Only one thing more can we do. Commend thyself to Allah, little sister. It is time for a moment of prayer."

Saya stood quietly, his head bowed slightly. Suddenly the thought occurred to him that both he and his sister might never see the light of a new day, might never again look upon the faces of their mother and father, might never again lounge in the comfortable goat-hair tent to sup a delicious meal. A look of panic crossed his face, and his eyes darted wildly in every direction. Fear was strong within Saya at this moment, but a new development fortunately forestalled his growing panic. Ja Mi Li, who had lain quietly only pricking up her ears at the howling of the jackals, now whinnied sharply. All her life she had roamed with the Bedouin horse herd, and the howl of the jackal was always followed by the sharp crack of the guards' rifles. No harm had ever come to the beautiful mare. But now a vagrant whim of nature caused a change in the desert wind. Dying down to almost a whisper, it suddenly switched direction and brought to Ja Mi Li's nostrils the scent of the jackal pack. Instinct told her that here was a great danger, a menace which might tear from her side the new-born colt which she knew she must protect. Rearing her body, she lunged to her feet, and her urgent voice brought the colt at once to her side. Now she turned to start her fleet way out of the oasis and away from the scent and the howls of the pack.

But Saya was too quick for her. At her first whinny and before she could jump to her feet, he was at her head, his strong brown hand reaching to grasp the halter on her head. As she turned to run, he twisted slightly to hold her, and his other hand softly stroked her sleek neck while his quiet voice reassured her. All fear was gone now from Saya's mind. His charges needed attention, and he gave it to them. He called to Nedda:

"Little sister . . . quickly, bring me the short rope which lies there."

Nedda jumped to her feet, snatched up the rope and ran to Saya's side. Commanding her to make a loop in the rope, Saya bent and lifted Ja Mi Li's foreleg. Then the boy suddenly threw his weight against Ja Mi Li's shoulder and, caught off balance, the mare toppled to the ground. In a trice, Saya had the loop of rope caught about both of her forelegs. He tied them strongly, and the beautiful mare was helpless. Nedda, surprised at Saya's sudden move, protested.

"Saya! The jackals come. You cannot leave Ja Mi Li helpless upon the ground!"

Saya shook his head.

"We must, Nedda," he answered. "She has caught the scent of the jackals. A panic is on her. If she is free, she will run, and the colt will run at her side. They will be pulled down by the jackal pack before they have run out of the oasis to the open desert. No, little sister, it is we who must protect Ja Mi Li and her baby."

The boy turned his attention now to the great stallion. Khala Hawa still lay quietly on the sand, but now his eyes were fully open and his tiny ears pricked up, twitching back and forth in whichever direction came the newest voice of a jackal. There was no more Saya could do. Motioning his sister to her seat beside the fire where the spare guns were ready to be thrust into his hands, Saya stood gazing over the protective square of fires, knowing that soon a flitting shadow would announce the beginning of the circle of death.

And then he saw it, the twin points of fire in the darkness, the malevolent eyes of a jackal reflecting the dancing firelight. The long rifle came up sharply, Saya took quick aim, and the sound of his shot echoed across the dunes to die in the distance. A sharp yelp came from the spot where the eyes had disappeared, and as though the little drama had been a signal, a thousand devils seemed to join in a chorus. Now the tiny group was ringed with shaggy yellow beasts, slavering in their desire to close with the dinner which seemed just beyond fang reach.

Now all pretense at secrecy was gone. One shaggy form after another ran close to the square outlined in the firelight only to be met by a burst of flame and the sharp crack of Saya's rifle. Many a yellow brute fell, to be instantly pounced upon by others of the pack and torn to shreds in moments. Nedda, her tiny arms moving like little pistons, her hands blistered from the hot gun barrels, reloaded the weapons as fast as Saya fired them. But the frenzy of the pack mounted. So near and yet so far! The scent of the helpless horses was strong in their nostrils. The scent of the new-born colt, whose flesh would be tender under their ripping fangs, tantalized them. Closer and closer the snarling beasts came until they skulked just beyond the fires, and so many of them were there that Saya could have fired blindly and not missed.

But the boy did not do this. Each time his rifle raised, he sighted carefully and made each bullet count. But there could be only one end. The flickering fires began to drop their flames lower and lower as the fuel burned away. There was no time to carry more to replenish them. And as the flames died, so did the warning heat, and closer and closer the circling jackals came to the fires, risking singed hair in the hope of reaching one of the animals. Nedda, her breath sobbing in her throat from the pain of blistered hands and fatigue, called to Saya:

"Brother . . . brother, the ammunition is gone. Only two more rifles can I load."

Saya, about to fire, dropped his rifle. With the one

in his hands, this meant that only three more shots were left to him. He turned quickly.

"Nedda, take up a fire brand. I will hold the jackals away. Run quickly to the nearest date palm and climb high. Stay there until the pack goes. They will go when . . ." his voice faltered. ". . . when they have finished eating."

But Nedda would not stir. She did take up the firebrand as Saya directed, but she held it firmly in her blistered little fists. Though tears ran down her powder-stained face, Nedda stood squarely beside her brother. Saya had no time to urge her, for the scurrying figures of the jackals came closer and closer. Now his last shot brought down a huge brute whose daring had brought him within the dying ring of fire. And just in time, for the jackal was about to launch himself at the frightened colt which cringed against its mother as she lay on the ground, still struggling to rise.

Saya slowly turned his rifle in his hands until he held it by the long barrel. The strongly made stock at the end of the barrel would make a fine club. Saya determined to bring it down on a few skulls before the pack dragged him to earth. There was nothing else but for him and Nedda to sell their lives as dearly as possible. The pack set up a fearful yapping now. Driven mad by the scent of the horses from whom they had been withheld and the taste of blood from their own fallen comrades, the jackals became progressively more daring. Now that the spurts of flame and the whining bullets which they feared had ceased, the jackals became braver. As suddenly as a sandstorm can blow up on the wide expanse of the desert, the pack drew together for the final rush which Saya knew would overwhelm his puny defenses. He turned to Nedda, thrust his knife into her hands, and commanded her to cut Ja Mi Li free, mount the mare and try to escape over the desert. Nedda, almost overcome with fatigue and fear, took the knife, stumbled towards the mare and fell in a faint beside the beautiful horse, still struggling with the bonds which held her on the ground. Saya spun about again to face the jackals. Spread in a fan, they started towards the boy, who stood alone between them and the tasty meal just beyond him. For his own part, Saya awaited a quick death. He no longer had hope for anything more but that, in dying, he could take with him a few more of the killers.

Then from behind him came a sound which Saya had never thought to hear again in this life, a sound which was like a clutching hand upon his heart. For what he heard was the shrill wild scream of the fighting stallion. Darting an almost frightened glance behind him the boy saw his great horse lunge to his feet! Saya was sure that Khala Hawa had leaped to his feet in the wild plunging which sometimes accompanies the death struggle of a horse, but this was far from the truth. It was Saya's own weariness and anxiety for his charges which had caused him to miss the great changes in his horse through the recent days. Disheartened because the horse continued to lie passively in the sand, despite his ministrations, Saya had failed to see what actually was happening.

Once the bullet was removed, and the infection which had started to race through the great body was stopped, Khala Hawa had continued to gain in strength. Aided by the gruel which Saya had managed to administer, the otherwise powerful body had already begun to replace the lost blood. Instinctively the big horse had continued to lie quietly conserving his strength as it slowly returned to him. All these things were factors, but there was still one more. In every living creature there is a reserve of strength which waits unsuspected, until a moment of emergency, to be drawn upon. Now, when instinct told the stallion that he must fight or die, his great heart called upon this reserve of strength, and sent him to his feet screaming his challenge out over the world of sand.

For a fraction of a second the stallion faltered, then steadying himself he moved to Saya's side to meet the jackal pack which was almost upon them! Now the great horse with a surge of effort, reared high on his hind legs and his tiny rock-hard forehooves flashed in the last of the firelight. A new glory came into Saya's heart! Here was the way for a Bedouin to die, fighting side by side with a great war-horse . . . a fighter worth ten men, or fifty jackals. From the boy's throat came the war-cry of the Bedouin:

"Allah il Allah! There is no God but Allah!"

They met the shock of the first drive together. The jackals in the fore of the pack suddenly confronted with the screaming, plunging stallion tried to stop or turn aside, but those coming behind pressed them on. Saya forgot his fear and his fatigue fell away from him. He was here, there, everywhere slashing with his clubbed rifle at the snarling faces thrust up to his. Soon the sturdy wooden stock of his rifle was smashed to bits, but the long steel barrel served as well.

As for Khala Hawa—now reared high on his hind legs, he would crash down into the thick of the pack, and in seconds two, three, four jackals would be crushed beneath his cutting blows. Then suddenly his hind legs would flash out to send in a high arc the lifeless body of a jackal which had skulked behind him hoping to ham-string the powerful hind legs of the great horse.

It is hard for either a man or a horse to know his full strength until in desperation he must call upon it. But here the boy, who a few moments earlier had been ready to drop from exhaustion, fought like a demon, and here the horse, dying perhaps of a grievous wound, became a fearful engine of destruction! Indeed, it is possible that Khala Hawa could have been more than a match for the jackal pack himself.

The boy and his horse did not look for help, but it came from an unexpected quarter. From a semi-darkness lighted only by the fires which were slowly flickering out, the early desert dawn broke over the dunes. Though no sign of the sun was to be seen, the half light of the first dawn broadened in moments until the light of what little fire remained was paled. It was enough for the jackal pack. Skulkers, hiders in the shadows, murderers by sneak attack, they had no stomach for the fighting of Saya and Khala Hawa in the light of day.

Nedda returned to consciousness just in time to see Saya swing his rifle barrel one last and futile time at a shaggy body which scurried out of his way to lope away into the desert after his retreating companions. She saw the great body of Khala Hawa shaking with the weariness which began to come over his weakened body, and she became aware of the knife in her hand. Quickly she slashed the rope which held the mare's forefeet, and as Ja Mi Li lunged to her feet to be instantly joined by her hungry and frightened colt, Nedda looked again to see Saya sink slowly to the ground, the rifle barrel now bent and twisted dropping from his nerveless fingers. Nedda ran to her brother's side puzzled and amazed, for this brave boy, this big brother, this protector . . . was sobbing softly.

"Saya, Saya . . . what is it? What happens? Where are the jackals? Why are you crying?"

The questions poured from the little girl. Saya could hardly speak, and at first he only pointed towards his great stallion. Nedda looked at the horse. Khala Hawa's head, hung so low that his silky muzzle, splashed with the blood of the jackals for which his sharp teeth had accounted, nearly touched the sand. His legs were spread wide apart to brace his powerful body. As Saya and Nedda watched, the once sturdy forelegs quivered as though they would buckle and let the body fall to the ground. A choked sob escaped the boy.

"See him, Nedda," he said. "He fought as might a thousand devils. He it was who saved us finally when the jackals rushed our camp. He has killed himself to save us. See him . . . he dies . . . standing on his feet."

A tear trickled down Nedda's streaked face. And she laid her tiny hand on the boy's arm.

"Go to him, Saya. He waits for you, I think."

Now it was the boy's turn to force trembling limbs to hold his weight. It was a struggle to rise, for his body felt as heavy as the sand on the desert floor. Finally he stood and for a moment supported himself with a hand on Nedda's shoulder. Then as he braced himself to walk to Khala Hawa's side, another strange thing happened. Slowly the great head of the stallion lifted, and the heavy muscles of the neck corded under the strain. But the head did come up, and the tiny ears did prick up, and the nostrils did flare as Khala Hawa sniffed the air. Then with feeble but sure steps, Khala Hawa moved slowly to the great pile of grass still stacked in the middle of the wrecked camp. Again the sleek head lowered, the silken muzzle buried in the sweet grasses, and with a contented nicker, Khala Hawa began to eat.

Saya was paralyzed with surprise for a moment. His mouth dropped open, but no words came. And then his voice was a shout:

"Nedda, Nedda! He feeds! Khala Hawa feeds!"

Nedda sensed the excitement but did not understand.

"Then he is hungry, Saya? That is good?"

"It is not the dying horse which feeds, little sister. The dying horse wants only to lie on the ground. It is the horse who will live until there are no years left to him by Allah. Who will go to eat when his body is ready to drop from weariness. Khala Hawa will live, Nedda . . . he will live!"

Nedda nodded happily then slipped quietly to the ground, her eyes fluttering closed in sudden slumber. Saya looked at her and was about to follow her example when he remembered. Khala Hawa would wish to drink after his meal and before he rested again. Saya searched in the wreckage of the camp until he found the water skin. Then he trudged towards the little spring with the slow steps which were all his tired body could manage. But the numbing pains in his body were gone now. They had long since been swallowed by the joy in his heart.

A NOTE ON THE TYPE

The text of this book is set in Caledonia, a Linotype face designed by W. A. Dwiggins, the man responsible for so much that is good in contemporary book design and typography. Caledonia belongs to the family of printing types called "modern face" by printers—a term used to mark the change in style of type-letters that occurred about 1800. It has all the hard-working feet-on-the-ground qualities of the Scotch Modern face plus the liveliness and grace that is integral in every Dwiggins "product" whether it be a simple catalogue cover or an almost human puppet.

The book was composed by H. Wolff, New York. Printed and bound by The Book Press Incorporated, Brattleboro, Vermont.